Leonard Chappelow

Six Assemblies

Ingenious conversations of learned men among the Arabians

Leonard Chappelow

Six Assemblies
Ingenious conversations of learned men among the Arabians

ISBN/EAN: 9783337279776

Hergestellt in Europa, USA, Kanada, Australien, Japan

Cover: Foto ©Andreas Hilbeck / pixelio.de

Weitere Bücher finden Sie auf **www.hansebooks.com**

· O R,

INGENIOUS CONVERSATIONS

O F

LEARNED MEN among the ARABIANS,

U P O N
A great Variety of ufeful and entertaining SUBJECTS;
formerly publifhed by the celebrated SCHULTENs in
Arabic and *Latin*, with large Notes and Obferva-
tions explaining feveral peculiar CUSTOMS, MAN-
NERS and IDIOMS of SPEECH amongft the Eaftern
People ; whereby much Light is thrown upon many
Paffages of SCRIPTURE, both of the OLD and NEW
TESTAMENT :

T O G E T H E R
With a COLLECTION of feveral PROVERBIAL SAYINGS
among the *Arabians*, with an Explanation of their
SINGULAR BEAUTY and PROPRIETY.

The Whole now *tranflated* into *Englifh*, with Improvements.

By LEONARD CHAPPELOW, B. D.
Arabic Profeffor in the *Univerfity* of *Cambridge*.

CAMBRIDGE:
Printed by J. ARCHDEACON, Printer to the UNIVERSITY ;
For MERRILL in Cambridge , and fold by JOHNSON & DAVEN-
PORT in Pater-Nofter-Row ; DODSLEY in Pall-Mall ; WHITE
in Fleet-Street ; and ROBSON in New Bond-Street, London ;
FLETCHER and PRINCE at Oxford ; and ETHERINGTON at
York.
M,DCC,LXVII.

TO THE RIGHT HONOURABLE

LORD MAYNARD.

My Lord,

PRESUMING on your Lordſhip's Candour, I flatter myſelf you will be ſo favourable as to excuſe the freedom I take in prefixing your name to theſe *Aſſemblies*. I ſhould not have done this, was I not ſatisfied, that being honoured by ſo worthy a name, they would meet with a more eaſy and gracious reception from the public. It may poſſibly be thought impertinent, ſhould I attempt to ſay any thing in regard to your Lordſhip's very amiable, religious character, which is ſo well eſtabliſhed, and ſo generally known to the world. How happy would it be for us, did all Gentlemen, thoſe eſpecially of Your Quality, take pleaſure in imitating ſo diſtinguiſhed an example.

THERE

DEDICATION.

THERE are many ferious, good thoughts of our *Mahometan*, in the enfuing *Tracts*; fuch as deferve no little admiration; and fuch, I am per-fuaded, every well-difpofed Chriftian will approve of, and think it no dif-honour to copy after for his own pri-vate ufe and advantage.

I am, my LORD,

Your Lordfhip's moft obedient,

humble Servant,

LEONARD CHAPPELOW.

PREFACE.

THE Six *Assemblies* here offered to the Public, are part of those *fifty* which were written in Arabic by *Hariri* of *Barsa*, a city in the kingdom of Babylon. His name at large is by the Arabians thus distinguished, *Abu Mohammed Alkasim Ebn Ali Ebn Mohammed Ebn Othman Al-Basri Al-Hariri:* or, more simply, *Ebno-'l Hariri: The son of a silk-merchant.* The time of his birth was in the year of *Hegirah,* [i. e. *Mahomet's flight* from *Mecca* to *Medinah*] 446: of his death about 516, or A. D. 1122. *Assemblies* in Arabic are called *makamaton,* viz. *sessions,* or *meetings;* such particularly as were appointed by learned men to examine and discourse on useful and edifying subjects. To each tract the Author ascribes a name, taken from a remarkable place or city where you are to suppose the discourse was held. For instance, that which hath the title of *Sananensis,* intimates that it was the subject of a friendly society at *Sanaa* in *Arabia Felix.* This *Assembly* [with several others] is opened under the feigned name of *Harith,* the son of *Hemmam.* The former signifying *an industrious man:* the latter, one who is *curious in observing* other peoples conduct of life. The province assigned to this person, is, to entertain you with the remarks he had made in the places through which he travelled; describing them in an elegant manner, and in such language as shews him to be a master of those talents which are the ornament of a polite scholar. He takes occasion to introduce an old man, by name *Abuzeid,* who presents himself to him in every city: a person of so much art, wit, and

a experi-

experience, as to aſſume what ſhape, or to appear in what poſture he pleaſed, agreeable to the
circumſtances of time or place, or the humours
of thoſe he happened to converſe 'with.   The
meeting with one of ſuch ſuperior qualities
proves to be a very lucky incident : for from the
diſcourſe that paſſed he receives many advantages, eſpecially thoſe which are inſtrumental in
promoting the comfort and happineſs of life.
To *his* taſte and humour the Author accommo-
dates himſelf in the eaſieſt manner, paying the
utmoſt deference to his judgement; eſteeming
him as a rare, uncommon example, worthy of
the moſt diligent imitation.   This conduct ex-
hibits to us a ſcene of much thought and pru-
dential contrivance : for with greater ſecurity to
himſelf, and with leſs odium from the public,
he acts the part of a general Cenſor; he ſatyrizes
the vices of thoſe men, which he perceived were
growing to an high degree of inſolence : no method, in his opinion, being ſo proper as that
which he purſues, to bring about a general re-
formation, and which is the great point he ſeems
to aim at.

The character which *Ebn Chalican,* an Arabian, [who died A. D. 1281] in his hiſtory of
Famous Men, draws of *Hariri,* is very ſingular
and excellent.   He deſcribes him as *the moſt
learned man of the age; peculiarly happy in the
compoſition of his Al-makamah ; written with ſo
much ſpirit and elegancy, that there you read the
language of the Arabians in it's higheſt perfection;
you are acquainted with their particular forms of
expreſſion, their proverbs, and the moſt intimate
terms contained in the Arab tongue.*   The natural
and valuable endowments which he was poſſeſſed
of, were the extraordinary gift of Providence,
to make, as it were, ſome compenſation for the
ſhortneſs of his ſtature, and the deformity of his
countenance : both which were ſo remarkable,
that

that he was an object of contempt to thofe who
were ignorant of his virtuous accomplifhments.
An inftance of this we have from the account of
a certain ftranger, who being informed of his
great abilities, determined to pay him a vifit,
with a view of receiving from him fome ufeful
and edifying inftructions. But as foon as he came
and caft his eye upon him, his warm expectations
grew cool, and all his hopes were immediately
fruftrated: for the very fight of that mean, uncommon figure, in which he appeared, altered
his opinion, and gave him fuch a diftafte, that
far from the thoughts of any improvement, his
refentment was fo quick as to defpife him to the
loweft degree. But yet to indulge his curiofity,
as if nothing that he could deliver would be of
any moment, he defired him to dictate what
would be worth his attention. To which *Hariri*
confented, and made this reply in verfe :

> *Thou'rt not the firft night-wand'rer,*
> *Deceiv'd by treach'rous moon-light:*
> *Nor the firft ftarv'd Purveyor,*
> *Pleas'd with the fpacious furface*
> *Of dunghill's outward verdure,*
> *The greedy eye attracting:*
> *When all within is naufeous.*
> *In choofing a companion,*
> *Thy choice, I find, directs thee*
> *To one of diff'rent afpect;*
> *For I am like old Moaïd,*
> *Deform'd in ev'ry member.*
> *Hear then what I fhall dictate;*
> *But let thine eye not fee me;*
> *For prejudice will fruftrate*
> *The wifeft, beft inftructions.*

At this unexpected anfwer the ftranger retired in
much confufion.

In the verfes above *Hariri* alludes to what was
commonly mentioned as a proverb, viz. *You may
hear Moaïd, but not look on him:* intimating, that

a great and noble ſoul may be lodged in a little, deformed body. For it is reported of him, when he had met with ſome contemptuous treatment from *Nooman* king of the *Hirenſes*, becauſe he was a dwarf in ſtature; with great ſedateneſs and coolneſs of temper he made this wiſe reply: *The real eſtimate of man conſiſts in two ſmall things belonging to him, The heart and the tongue.*

The inſtructions which are dictated in the following piece, &c. and the rules laid down for the good conduct of life, are ſhort and conciſe: and indeed conſidering the ſmallneſs of the Tracts, they could not be otherwiſe. But you will find them delivered in ſuch nervous, ſtrong terms, that they cannot but ſtrike the imagination, and have a very powerful effect on the mind of every ſerious, well-diſpoſed reader. The follies and exceſſes, in which the unthinking part of mankind indulge themſelves, are expoſed in a decent, proper manner. You ſee the genius of a prudent, diſcreet Satyriſt, without that unbecoming language, which offends a tender, chaſt ear. The beauty of any virtue, every body knows, appears to greater advantage, and ſhines in a brighter luſtre, when the deformity of the oppoſite vice is repreſented to you by way of contraſt. This is the method our Author purſues; and a very commendable one we muſt allow it: for by this repreſentation our thoughts are more ſenſibly affected, and raiſed to the higheſt admiration of ſuch ornaments as ſet off the one, and fall to the loweſt opinion of that baſeneſs which accompanies the other. For inſtance, when he would ſhew the folly of that perſon who thinks himſelf very ſecure, ſo long as he carries on his villainous intrigues, and eſcapes the view of the world: not apprehending that his deepeſt ſecrets are diſcovered by a ſuperior power:—How affecting is the manner of his addreſs to ſuch a ſelf-deceiver! *viz. So artfully contrived, as thou imagineſt, are*

thy

thy actions, that even thy neighbour is ignorant of them, when at the same time thou art exposed to the eye of thy great Obferver. *Thou art very folicitous that thy fervant fhould know nothing of thy projects, when the moft private defign is public to thy* Mafter. From hence we learn that human nature, though fadly corrupted, give it but time and leifure to confider and look into itfelf, foon difcovers it's own weaknefs and imperfections, as well as thofe of other men's: and that when once it begins to be truly ferious, it muft be the fame, in many refpects, in all people of what country or profeffion foever. A farther and more advantageous inftruction occurs to us, that there is a principle implanted in us, fo excellent in it's kind, and fo worthy of our Creator's divine power, that fome pains muft be taken, violent meafures ufed, before we can totally efface that beauteous image, which notwithftanding the ftrongeft oppofition, is ever ready to reprefent itfelf to us. By a juft and unprejudiced way of thinking we fhall be able to difcover that our rational endowments are not given us with a liberty to abufe them by exceffes of any kind: and that doing injury to thefe, is doing injury to human nature, as well as our gracious Benefactor. Such without queftion were the fentiments of the Author of the *Affemblies:* whofe cool, virtuous thoughts directed him to expofe, and if poffible, to correct, the common and popular errors, which occafion fo much difturbance and confufion in the world. That his hopes and expectations of happinefs did not center *here,* is evident from the queftion he puts to the unthinking Senfualift, viz. *Is thy grave to be the dormitory, where thou art only to lie down, and take thy noon-day repofe? What anfwer wilt thou make when called to a ftrict examination? At thy departure hence, when thou fhalt return to God, and appear at the bar of his juftice, Who fhall be*

art

an advocate to plead for thee? Here let me aſk,
Shall not this *Mahometan* riſe up in judgement a-
gainſt thoſe ſelf-opinionated reaſoners, who would
make you believe, they want no farther inſtructions but what their own faculties ſuggeſt; and
that without any advocate they are able to plead
their own cauſe even before God himſelf. Our
Author, by the religion he profeſſed, as the *Alcoran* taught him, believed in Jeſus Chriſt, ſo
far as he was a great Prophet ſent by God : and
no doubt but the prejudice of education hindered
him from carrying his belief higher. Had he
been bleſſed with the ſame opportunities of
knowing the doctrines of Chriſtianity, which
our modern unbelievers are favoured with ; I am
perſuaded he would have diſtinguiſhed himſelf
as a faithful and ſincere convert ; that he would
have lived and died a Chriſtian in the beſt and
trueſt ſenſe. The moral precepts which he gives
in the following Tracts are delivered with ſuch
conſideration and judgement, ſuch ſerioufneſs and
piety, that every reader muſt ſurely be convinced,
his attention was not to amuſe only, but to teach
the ignorant, to reform the vicious, and to eſtab-
liſh thoſe principles, which, if improved as they
ought to be, might be greatly inſtrumental in
promoting both the preſent and future happineſs
of mankind.

I muſt not conclude this Preface without acquainting the reader that this *Aſſembly*, entitled
Sananenſis, was firſt tranſlated and publiſhed by the
learned *Golius* with the Arabic and Latin verſion,
and with only a few notes, at *Leyden*, in 4to,
1656; but re-publiſhed with much larger notes,
by that great Maſter of Arabic, *Albert Schultens*,
at *Franequer*, 4to, 1731. To which he added
five more, purſuing the ſame method that he
took in the firſt, of explaining difficult paſſages
from the Scholiaſt, &c.

6

My

My attempt to tranſlate thoſe which are publiſhed, will, I hope, in ſome meaſure be not
only acceptable, but inſtructive to an Engliſh
reader; for he will ſoon be convinced that notwithſtanding our Author was a *Mahometan,* yet
he had thoroughly ſtudied the prevailing force
of human paſſions; and that he was maſter of
very rich talents, ſufficient to expoſe the follies
and vices, to which mankind in general, of all
profeſſions whatſoever, are by nature too much
inclined.

The Arabians are remarkably diſtinguiſhed
for many wiſe and ſententious expreſſions: I
have therefore ſelected ſome of their *proverbs*
which I find interſperſed in the *Aſſemblies* ; and
have occaſionally explained ſeveral Texts of
Holy Scripture.

TESTI-

HARIRÆUS HIZJRÆ, *id eſt,* Refugii Muhammedici, *anno* 446 *natus,* 516 *denatus, eo vixit ævo; quod politioribus inter Arabas literis pluri-mum floreret. Eamque in biſce ipſe promeruit laudem, ut earundem in Aſia & Africa ſtudioſis in præſentem ex-inde diem commodior vix alius habeatur Author, à quo proprietatem linguæ, ſimulque copiam ac elegantiam addiſ-cant.* Golii Præf. *ad* Conſeſſum *primum.*

Scriptor ille ſemper novus, ſemper recens, ea polluit vena, quæ uſque et uſque inter manandum creſcat, ſeque ipſa ditior jugiter, uberiorque evadat. Nihil propterea legiſſe, nihil intelligere inter eruditiores Arabes cenſetur, qui Haririum non contriverit, ac velut in ſuccum & ſanguinem converterit. Schultens Præf. *ad* Conſeſſum *quartum.*

Hariri *compoſa un ouvrage ſous le titre de* Mecâmat *lequel eſt eſtimé un chef d' œuvre d' éloquence Arabique. Il contient cinquante diſcours, ou eſpeces de déclamations ſur differens ſujets de morale, & chaque de ces diſcours porte le nom du lieu où il a été recité,* Herbelot Biblio-theque Oriental, *in voce* Hariri.

SIX ASSEMBLIES,

OR,

INGENIOUS CONVERSATIONS.

ASSEMBLY I,

ENTITLED

SANANENSIS.

HARITH the fon of *Hemmam* hath tranfmitted to us the following Affembly.—Having *mounted* my *travelling camel* and the courfe I purfued carried me a great diftance from my *native friends*; I was reduced to a *neceffitous condition*. The *viciffitudes of fortune*, like the boifterous waves of the fea, when they diftrefs the fhipwrecked mariner, with the fame fwiftnefs as an arrow difcharged from a bow, preffed upon me with fuch an impetuous force; clouded me with fo much error and confufion, that they *haftened my paffage* as far as *Sanaa* in *Arabia Felix*. When I entered the city, my *pockets* were *exhaufted*; my *poverty* very *remarkable*; not having fo much as one day's fuftenance left, nor a fingle morfel in my bag. In fhort, my bowels, for want of refrefhment, were fo contracted, that I was like an old manfionhoufe without any furniture; ready to fall by every blaft of wind. You might compare me to a decayed leathern quiver, or a fhepherd's fhrivelled pouch; which being empty of provifions, he fhakes and expofes to the open air. This demand of an immediate fupply obliged me, like an impotent, wild ftroller, to pafs through every part of the city. In my circuit

A   from

from one ftreet to another, I moved as a bird, which
flies fwiftly round the furface of water, with a defire to drink, but yet afraid to attempt it. My foot-
fteps, in the feveral avenues where I directed my
courfe, refembled thofe of an herd of cattle; when to
fatisfy their hunger, or to quench their thirft, they
eagerly prefs forward to the pafture, or place of watering. Mine eyes *entertained themfelves* without any reftraint, like darts piercing through every part of *my
excurfion.* My intention was to find out a perfon of fo
much honour and generofity, that I might communicate to him with the utmoft freedom the circumftances of my diftrefs:— or, if I failed in that point,
a man of letters; whofe agreeable countenance might
diffipate my anxiety, which was fo grievous, that it
hindered me almoft from taking my breath: and
whofe elegant converfation might *afford* me fome
pleafing refrefhment. During this contemplation, I
found I was advanced even to the extremity of my
circuit; the feveral inquiries I made, int he tendereft
manner I was able, proving fo aufpicious, as to conduct me to a numerous affembly of men, crowding
one upon another, and raifing their voices in much
weeping and lamentation. Having forced my way
through this multitude, (with the fame difficulty as
if I was entering into the center of a thick wood,) to
know the caufe that drew fo many tears from their
eyes; in the midft of the circle I efpied a perfon of a
lean, meagre vifage, furnifhed with all the *apparatus*
neceffary for a religious itinerant. The words that
he fpoke were uttered in the fame complaining accent
that you hear at a funeral; in fome meafure refembling the tremulous, tinkling found of a *bow,* as foon
as the arrow is difcharged. The fentences he pro-
nounced were delivered in rhymes, and with fuch exquifite fweetnefs of language, that one might call
them *rhymes fet with jewels of eloquence.* And the
reproofs he expreffed, fo full of fatyr and threatning
feverity, that they affected the ears of his audience to
a great degree. The croud that ftood round him
                                                        confifted

confifted of various ranks and orders of people; fo clofely united, that you might compare them to an halo, or circle about the moon; or, to the flowers of palms, or fruits of dates; which like fœtus's for a while lie concealed in the grand repofitory of nature. It was with no little pains I advanced nearer him, that I might be edified from his *falutary inftruⱸions*, and colleⱸ fome of his ftriking *obfervations*. I then heard his voice diftinⱸly, when he had raifed it to the higheft pitch; fpeaking with the fame degree of volubility and eagernefs, as when the fwift courfer runs and contends for the prize in the Circus. The words that he uttered were feemingly an *extempore oration*; flowing from him with fuch eafe as to require no premeditated thought; but in fo loud and clamourous a tone, as one hears from a camel, when bit with the ftinging Breez.

To his audience he thus addreffed himfelf: — O thou, of what ftation or rank foever, who without the leaft reftraint indulgeft thyfelf in thofe paffions which the petulant infolence of youth is ever ready to fuggeft; and by a clofe attention to the importunate exceffes of luftful pleafures, art as much difordered in mind with the fplendor of thy happinefs, as one, who by keeping his eyes for a long time fixed on the brightnefs of the fun, is affeⱸed with dizzinefs, and deprived even of fight. Thou, I fay, who *fuffereft thy thoughts* to be tranfported with vain and falfe imaginations: who like a ftubborn, refraⱸory horfe, that fhakes his rider, not yielding to the check of his rein, rufheft headlong into *thy follies*; deviating from what is right, with a ftrong propenfity to thy *ludicrous*, criminal converfation: How long wilt thou feduce thyfelf by conftantly perfifting in error, and indulge thy vicious tafte by tranfgreffing the rules of truth and juftice? How long wilt thou labour to rife to the utmoft height of pride and vain glory; and not ceafe to engage in fuch wanton, effeminate pleafures, as divert the mind from whatever is of any ferious moment? by this obftinacy of temper thou art con-

tending

tending with one who is thy *superior*, and hath an absolute command over thee. Thy dishonourable conduct makes thee so audacious as to live in opposition to him, from whom no secret is concealed. So artfully contrived, as thou imaginest, are thy actions, that even thy neighbour is ignorant of them: when at the same time thou art exposed to the eye of thy great Observer. Thou art very solicitous that thy servant should know nothing of thy projects, when the most private design is public to thy Master. What? art thou so weak as to suppose the most prosperous condition will be of any advantage, when the time is drawing near for thy departure out of this world? will the richest treasures be able to deliver thee, when thy own works have occasioned thy destruction? Or, thy repentance make so full a satisfaction, as to answer all those questions that will be demanded of thee, concerning the numerous *errors* thou hast been guilty of? is it thy opinion that they who have been thy *companions*, though never so many, and their affections never so strong, can be of any service to thee at the *day of Judgement*? Let me advise thee to *rectify* thy progress, and without delay to think of some remedies that may remove thy distemper, and check the *impetuous course* of thy transgressions. This may be done by laying a restraint on the soul, and confining it's extravagant motions within just and proper limits; because it is the most powerful enemy thou hast to engage with. When death gives the fatal stroke, is thy last period then determined? what preparation hast thou made for that solemn time? thy grey hairs are monitors sufficient to possess thee with an awful terror. And what excuses wilt thou form in vindication of thyself? is thy grave to be the dormitory, where thou art only to lie down, and take thy noon-day repose? what answer wilt thou make, when called to a strict *examination?* at thy departure hence, when thou shalt return to God, and appear at the bar of his justice; who shall be an advocate to plead for thee? thou hast lived long enough to awake

out

out of fleep. But inftead of vigilance, thy time hath been confumed in a voluntary flumber. The beft advice to reform thee hath not been wanting; but this thou haft obftinately *refifted*. Examples of the moft engaging nature have been propofed for thy imitation: but fuch a degree of blindnefs haft thou indulged, as not in the leaft to be affected by them. Truth and righteoufnefs have appeared to thee in their fimple, naked drefs: but to oppofe and difpute againft them, thou haft *exerted* the utmoft of thy power. Death hath given thee frequent calls to recollect thy actions: but to fo little purpofe, that thou art defirous of having no remembrance of them. To communicate to the relief of other men's indigent circumftances, thou haft been favoured with all the opportunities imaginable: but thefe thou haft greatly neglected. Thy love of money hath been fo ftrong and prevailing, that to the beft and wifeft inftructions, both of the Coran, and the traditions of our anceftors, concerning religion and fubjects truly divine, (which fhould be valued as the higheft treafure:) thou haft given the preference of heaping up abundance of riches. And to gratify thy pride, thou hadft rather diftinguifh thyfelf by raifing a ftately, expenfive building, than by doing a fingle act of beneficence and charity. In thy travelling expeditions, fo far from being conducted by one who would fhew thee the right way; thou choofeft to take a different courfe, and appear as a ftarved mendicant, a common beggar for an alms: and to be pointed at for wearing a loofe, flowing garment, rather than to merit a reward by performing fome bufinefs of weight and importance. Thy heart is fo immoderately fixed on receiving large and valuable prefents, that they influence thy affections more than the ftated folemn *times of prayer*. And trafficking for *dowries*, to be paid at certain times, and on certain conditions is more eligible with thee, than the appointing any feafon for charitable diftributions. So great an Epicure! that thou haft a ftronger relifh for tafting variety of difhes, ferved up in different

forms

forms and colours, than for entertaining thy felf with devout and heavenly meditations. Such a lover of foolifh jefting, that cuftom hath made it more familiar to thee than even reading the Coran. Thou art ready enough to command others what is juft and equitable; but thy felf remarkable for violating things facred, and doing that which is ftrictly forbidden. And whatever is of vitious infection, thou canft eafily difcourage: but doft not preferve thyfelf pure and free from it. Thy counfel to others, is, to keep at the greateft diftance from injuftice ; when with the ftrongeft paffion thou even lufteft after it. And as to men, thou art more afraid of *them*, than thou art of God ; who fhould be the principal object of thy fear. He then fpoke in verfe :

Curfe *on the man, whofe* eager mind *is fix'd*
  On prefent worldly profpects:
Mov'd with exceffive paffionate defires,
  His reafon's quite abandoned.
Did he but know the world's true eftimate :
  'Tis fmall, not worth purfuing.

His voice, which he had uttered in a very high ftrain, now *ceafed :* and the *flow of tears,* which he difcharged in great abundance, being dried up ; he gathered his outer-garment under his arm, and fixed his ftaff in the travelling pofition. But when the crouded audience, whofe *eyes* were intenfly *fixed* on him, perceived that he was changing his pofture, and *making a motion to rife and remove from his place* ; every one of them put his hand into *his pocket,* and made him *large prefents,* addreffing him in this manner : Whenever thy neceffities make their demand ; or when thou art difpofed to fupply thofe of thy friends and companions ; keep this in referve to lay out as thy judgement directs. Having received their generous offerings, he looked upon them with his eyes contracted in fuch a manner, as if he was afhamed to be enriched with fo large a bounty : returning them thanks in the higheft expreffions of gratitude. His
defign

design was to withdraw himself from them so as they might not know what course he intended to pursue. And he gave a strict charge to those who would have followed him, to go, some one way, some another, on purpose to keep them ignorant where the place of habitation was, to which he should retire. But *Harith* the son of *Hemmam*, notwithstanding that injunction, gives this account of himself: *viz.* Being determined to know his motions, I followed him at a proper distance, diverting mine eyes in such a manner that he should not suspect my design. I observed every step he took, with such care, that he could not possibly see me, till at last he came to the point he was aiming at: and that was a cave, into which he made a quick and precipitate entrance. I indulged him in his own way without interruption, till he had put off his shoes, and washed his feet. Then rushing hastily upon him, I found him sitting over-gainst one who was his disciple, entertaining themselves in much satisfaction, with bread made of the finest flour, with a roasted kid, and a vessel of wine before them. ——— Oh, sir, said I, is it here I find you? is that the place where all your doctrine terminates? is this to be the subject whenever your name is mentioned? At this unexpected surprise his voice faltered; his spirits sunk; he sighed and groaned in hollow, deep sounds, and was very near breaking out into the highest extreme of anger and fury. He looked upon me with such a severe stern countenance, that I really apprehended he would shew his resentment by some very great *insult*. But as soon as the fire, which he had kindled within him, was abated, and the flame, ready to break out, extinguished; he repeated these verses:

T' appear in robes of *richest* sable,
With all the ornaments of splendor,
In hopes *of ease and full enjoyment,*
Was once my large, ambitious *prospect.*

T' accumulate the vilest treasure,
My dext'rous book was always ready.

A 4   I

I cast my net, and took the refuse,
As well as fish of choicest value.

My private judgement was devoted
To the severity of fortune :
For by my resolute evasions,
I forc'd my way through dens of lions.

Not that I fear'd the artful projects
She form'd to flatter and deceive me :
Nor did I dread her frowns, or tremble,
Whene'er she shook her rod of vengeance.

My soul, tho' eagerly pursuing
Variety of life's enjoyments,
Did not divert me to such objects,
As would have sacrific'd mine honour.

But had th' unerring scales of justice
Been poiz'd impartially by fortune ;
To men of vitious dispositions,
Dominion she'd ne'er entrusted.

Having expreffed himfelf in this elegant poetry, he
invited me to come near them and partake of the entertainment : but I refufed his invitation, neither did I
choofe to make a longer ftay. I then with all the
earneftnefs imaginable, fignified both by mine eyes
and countenance, turned haftily to his difciple, and
faid ; I conjure thee by the almighty God, (to whom
thy folemn addreffes are made to defend thee from
evil) that thou fatisfy me, who this perfon is? Without any hefitation he immediately anfwered me ; This
is *Abuzeid* of *Serugium*, truly diftinguifhed by the
titles of *The Lamp of ftrangers*, and *Crown of the learned*. After this I retired to the place from whence I
came, being affected with the higheft admiration of
the incidents I happened to meet with.

NOTES

N O T E S

O N

A S S E M B L Y I.

E N T I T L E D

S A N A N E N S I S.

PAG. 1. *Mounted.* The Arabic language is so full and expressive, that the verb which is used in this place signifies, *to travel with a male camel when fit for the rider.*

Ib. *Travelling Camel: gáribo-'l-igterábi*, literally, *the back of my Camel, in order for a journey.* You observe here how the two Arabic words in sound correspond with each other. This method is pursued through the whole assembly. I shall not trouble the reader with many instances of this kind: nor shall I imitate the author in my translation. To attempt it, might be looked upon as a piece of pedantry: and indeed our English tongue will not admit of it. His design is so far laudable, as by this means one sees how great a genius he had for the poetry of his own times, and how extensive and copious is the Arabic language.

Ib. *Native friends:* expressed elegantly in the original, viz. *al-atrábo:* such as are descended from the same *toráb: soil* or *earth.* In reference to which is the Arabic for a *necessitous condition:* viz. *al-mátrabah:* because poverty makes a man cleave to *the earth,* or *dust.* From hence is that form of imprecation among the Arabians: " Let both thy hands *be filled with dust.* i. e. May nothing good attend thee!"

Ib.

Ib. *Vicissitudes of fortune, hastened my passage, táw wahat bi tahwáyibo-'l-zámáni: Fluctuarunt me fluctus fortunæ.* There is a peculiar beauty in the Arabic: For the radix *taha* is applied not only to *floods*, but to the uncertain motions of an arrow when discharged : and to any *confusion*, or *error* that happens to us. These several interpretations are hinted at in the version.

Ib. *Sanaa*, the metropolis of *Arabia Felix*; once a royal city built in a very artificial manner, as the word itself denotes, viz. *To form any thing with art and industry*. Like *Damascus* it was enriched with variety of trees and waters.

Ib. *My pockets exhausted: cháwiyo-'l-wifádi, vacuus loculos. cháwa* denotes *an empty house, ready to fall:* and *the belly contracted for want of victuals. wifádou: leathern quivers: shepherds bags.*

Ib. *My poverty remarkable: bádiyo-'l-infadi: conspicuus inopia:* literally, *taken notice of for my shaking.* Intimating such poverty, as when a traveller, his whole viaticum being spent, *turns and shakes his bag.*

Pag. 2. *Entertained*, &c. Arab. *I foraged through the pastures of my vibrations*, i. e. as the scholiast writes, " Those places where mine eye by contemplating fed, or entertaining itself with the utmost freedom : " Or, where mine eye as I passed, took a quick view like the vibrating motion of lightning. This corresponds with the Latin, *vibrans intuitus : nictantia fulmina : nictantes oculi.* The Arab. Poet, cited by *Tebrizius* in allusion to that liberty which the eye indulges in making proper observations; particularly such as have regard to those who are lovers of riches, and envy others who are richer than themselves; gives us this elegant satyr: [Notes on *Abu Temmam*'s Hamasa, or *warlike fortitude*; consisting of a large collection of poetry, from several poets both before and after the time of *Mahomet*.]

> *Feed but thine eyes with freedom round his tents;*
> *The only objects that present themselves,*
> *Are wealth and envy.*

Ib,

Ib. *Excurſion*: Arab. *In my going and returning:* or, *through the ſpaces of my morning and evening forage.* *To go out in the morning, and return in the evening,* is the ſame with the Arabians as *regularly to diſcharge all the offices of life.* They apply thoſe words to a farther uſe, in deſcribing the reſemblance of a ſon to a father: *viz.* " He does not forſake him either *morning,* or *evening.*" This phraſe of *going* and *coming* is uſed in Hebrew to ſignify the happineſs that attends obedience to divine commands: as *Deut.* xxviii. 6, 7. "Bleſſed ſhalt thou be when thou *comeſt in,* and when thou *goeſt out.*" It is likewiſe applied to the incapacity both of old age and youth. " I can no more *go out,* and *come in,* ſaith *Moſes,* ch. xxxi, 2. *i. e.* I am now entered into the laſt ſtage of life, and therefore no further ſervice can be expected from me." And when it pleaſed God to give him warning of his death, ch. xxvii. 16, 17. he made this requeſt, " Let the Lord ſet a man over the congregation which may *go out* before them, and which may *bring them in.*" On the contrary, *Solomon* 1 *Kings* iii. 7. addreſſes himſelf to God in theſe words; " Thou haſt made thy ſervant king; I am a little child, I know not how to *go out,* or *come in.*" *i. e.* My youth and want of experience are ſuch, that I am not capable of diſcharging the duties which are incumbent on ſo high a ſtation.

Ib. *Communicate,* &c. The Arabic is ſo expreſſive as to intimate, *To whom I might ſhew the ſkin of my face, which by my frequent cuſtom of petitioning for ſubſiſtence had changed it's natural modeſt complexion, like a ſilken garment that by long uſe is grown thread-bare, and loſt all it's former beauty.*

Ib. *Afford,* &c. Arab. Who from ſome place or other might fetch me water to quench my parching thirſt.

Ib. *Apparatus,* &c. viz. *A linen garment, a roſary with beads, to take the number of prayers, a ſtaff, a cup,* &c.

A bow : mirnánon : from *rána, to make a tinkling ſound.* To which the poet *Ibn El-Roumi* alludes, ſpeaking of the mutual effect of love :

So

So ſtrong the influence on her lover's thoughts!
That loud's the am'rous ſound of his complaints.
But when affeɭed with this anxious pain,
In mutual compaſſion ſhe laments.
Like the ſtrong bow that wounds the tim'rous prey;
In ſympathy you hear it's rattling noiſe.

Pag. 3. *Inſtruɭions:* Arab. That I might requeſt of him a torch, or fire to ſupply my focus; or, kindle *mine* from *his* fire.

Ib. *Obſervations.* Arab. *Singular jewels*; or, *particles of gold*; ſuch as in pearls are inſerted between each ſtone, to increaſe both their beauty and value.

Ib. *Extemp. irtegálon: Orations or verſes delivered extempore;* from *rágala, pedibus adſtitit:* [*ſtans pede in uno.*]

Ib. *Loud,* &c. The ſcholiaſt *Tebleb* obſerves that *ſhakáshiko,* uſed here, implies ſuch a redoubled braying noiſe as a ſtallion camel makes when in high ſpirits, with the utmoſt ſtretch of his lungs; and that from hence Orators, by dilating and diſtorting their mouths, are called *Maſters of the lungs.*

Ib. *Suffereſt,* &c. The original here is expreſſed in the eaſtern ſublime: viz. *Thou who letteſt the garments of thy pride hang looſe:* alluding to the *fooliſh pride* of thoſe days [Arab. *chala: ſtulte ſuperbire*] of wearing a flowing train that dragged and ſwept the ground: a faſhion too much adopted by our Engliſh ladies.

Ib. *Thy ſelf, thy thoughts, thy follies, thy ludicrous,* &c. inſtead of which, the Arabic is, *himſelf, his thoughts, his follies, his ludicrous,* &c. viz. Thou who *ſuffereſt himſelf,* &c. This tranſition of perſon is peculiar to the eaſtern tongues, and we find it frequently in holy ſcripture: as *Job* xviii. 4. He teareth himſelf in his anger, for, *thou teareſt thyſelf,* &c. We meet with ſuch paſſages in the *Pſalms;* particularly in that remarkably divine compoſition of the 104th. *viz.* Thóu, O Lord, *árt very great — art clothed — who covereſt — who ſtretcheſt,* but in ℣. 3, &c. *Who layeth* the beams — *who maketh* the clouds — *who walketh — who maketh*

maketh his angels — *who laid* the foundation, and in
ỳ. 6, &c. *Thou coveredſt* it — at *thy rebuke*, &c. This
change is obſervable through the whole Pſalm. From
which I think we may draw this concluſion; That the
way of reading, or ſinging, this and other *Pſalms* of
the ſame kind, was for the greater ſolemnity by
voices alternate. Vid. *Pſ.* xviii. 25, & 145.

. Pag. 4. *Superior*, &c. Arab. *Who takes faſt hold of
the forelock. i. e.* To whoſe [God's] power and dominion thou art as ſubjeɛt, as a ſlave, or a beaſt is to his
maſter, who lays hold on, turns and direɛts them
which way ſoever he pleaſes.

. Ib. *Errors*, &c. Arab. *When thy foot by ſtumbling hath
deceived thee.* A phraſe that we often read in ſcripture, relating to unſteddy ſinful conduɛt. *Pſal.* xxxviii.
16. *When my foot ſlippeth, they magnify themſelves.*
On the contrary, *Job* xxiii. 11. *My foot hath held his
ſteps.* Correſpondent to which is *Mahomet's* petition,
Alcor. iii. 147. *Lord, pardon our offences, and ſtrength-
en our feet.*

Ib. *Companions:* Arab. A ſociety, properly
ſpeaking, of ten men, ſupported by unjuſt means,
and dividing the ſpoil, by caſting lots into ten portions. Theſe portions are named *a'ſháron*, and the
ſociety itſelf, *ma'ſharon.*

Ib. *Day of Judgement.* Arab. *When the time or place
of the aſſembly ſhall conſtrain thee.* In the lxiv ch. of
the *Alcoran* ỳ. 10. we read, " God will gather you
together at the day of the *congregation*; [the laſt
Judgement] *that* being the day of *mutual deceit:*
[from which the chapter takes it's title] ſo called, ſay
the Arab. Commentators, *Gelaleddinus* and *Jahias*,
becauſe the believers [*Mahometans*] ſhall then de-
fraud the Infidels [ſuch as do not believe in *Mahomet*]
by taking thoſe ſeats in Paradiſe, together with their
families, which they would have poſſeſſed, had they
been of the number of the faithful. Theſe ſhall have
their portion in Paradiſe; thoſe in raging fire.

Ib. *To rectify*, &c. Or, as the words intimate, To
take

take the fame fteps as if thou wert going to a facred
folemnity at the temple of *Mecca.*

Ib. *Impetuous courfe:* Blunt [*fhabátan*] *the edge* of
thine iniquity.   A remarkable figure, as *Schultens* ·
writes : for the word denotes *a fharp-pointed fpear* ;
and particularly, *the fting of a fcorpion.* Not only
wicked and unrighteous men, but virulent expreffions, or facts, are by the Arabians compared to fcorpions.—When they would defcribe a perfon of an in-
famous character, they fay, *His fcorpions creep,* i. e.
avoid him as much as poffible; for if you affociate
with him he will do you fome fecret mifchief.

Ib. *Examination :* Golius [*Lexic.* rad. *nácira*] fup-
pofes an allufion is made to that fcrutiny, when the
Manes of deceafed perfons are to be *examined* by the
two angels *Necir* and *Moncir,* who are appointed for
that office.

Pag. 5. *Refifted: tekaáfta.* Thou haft been as ftubborn as a camel, whofe breaft, when provoked, fwells,
and his back finks.   But *ákafo: gibbofus:* from the
fame root, is, in a good fenfe applied to a man *grave
and fteddy in his purpofes. To true glory and honour,*
that is not fubject to any one's bondage.   Poetically,
to a long extended night.

Ib. *Exerted: maraîta: ftrinxifti. Haft ftrained thy
felf. Schultens* obferves here, that inftead of [*Ifai.* iii.
8.] their tongue and their doings are againft the
Lord, *le maroth, to provoke* the eyes of his glory ; we
fhould take the Arab. interpretation ; viz. *ad oculos
ejus gloriofos perftringendos* ; *to dazzle the eyes of his glory.*

Ib. *Times of prayer. Mahomet* [*Alcor.* xi. 115.] enjoins
his followers, to be conftant in their prayers, *at the
extremities of the day, and in the former part of the
night.* i. e. Morning and evening, *and when night approaches.* But their times of prayer are when *the day
breaks :* when *the fun rifes : at noon : in the afternoon :
at funfet. Gol.* Not.

Ib. *For Dowries.* i. e. For purchafing thofe funis of
money which the husband engages to pay his intended wife in cafe of a divorce, or at the time of death.

Ib.

Pag. 6. *Curse : Tábban.* An abbreviation of "Let God inflict *tábban, evil* on him! from *tábba, to cut.* Let his hands *tábbat, be cut off!* is an imprecation of the same kind.

Ib. *Eager mind,* &c. To aggravate the folly of too much anxiety, the author expresses himself in the Arab. verses above, in an elegant manner by three words taken from the radix *tsábba :* signifying, *to pour out like water* ; *to be deeply in love* ; *to drink the small remnant* of a vessel when it is almost exhausted. As if *the man of this world,* in his motions is as impetuous, as water let loose from confinement : his affection for present enjoyments strong as the most violent passion of love : and after all his labour finds his portion of happiness to be very small.

Ib. *Wordly prospects : Dónya : This present life,* or the riches belonging to it. *Mahomet*'s doctrine *Alcor.* xxix. 64. is very just, viz. *al-bayáwto al-dónya,* &c. *as to this present world,* it is a mere jest and ridicule : but the life to come, that is life indeed. *Ab Farajius* faith of *Abu Ali* a liberal physician; The women applied to him because of *donyáho : his riches.* Hist. Dynat. p. 457.

Ib. *His voice,* &c. *ceased.* Arab. *He laid his dust :* i. e. as the scholiast explains it ; his voice had been so loud that it was like a storm, which raises thick clouds of dust and smoke.

Ib. *Flow of tears :* literally, *Flow of juice squeezed out. Honey* the Arabians say, is *juice* squeezed from bees. *Rain, juice* from the clouds.

Ib. *Eyes fixed.* Arab. Whose quick-sighted eyes like darts pierced him.

Ib. *Making a motion to rise: Te-báffoza.* This word is so full as to express, *inftitit pedum digitis, erectâ superiore corporis parte, depressâ inferiore.* Or, what the Latins say, *coxim sedere :* signifying that posture in which travellers in the East use to refresh themselves ; viz. *incoxare se,* rather than *discumbere* vel *assidere.* Thus the Israelites were enjoined to eat the passover, *Exod.* xii. 1. with their loins girded, shoes

on

on their feet, ſtaffs in their hand, and *be-bhippazou*, in haſte. But though the word, as *Schultens* writes, may include *haſte*; yet it more immediately refers to that *poſture of body* above mentioned. So that this conſideration may determine the controverſy; whether the Iſraelites in Egypt celebrated the paſſover, *ſtanding*, or *ſitting*.

Ib. *Remove from his place*, literally, in the aſtronomers language, *decline from his center:* being placed in the middle of a numerous people.

.Ib. *His pocket.* Arab. *the plait*, or *fold of his garment.*

Ib. *Large preſents.* From the Arabic we underſtand, their liberality was ſuch, that it might be compared to water freely poured into a bucket, in order to fill it.

. Pag. 7. *Inſult.* The original alludes to an Arab. phraſe: viz. *Such an one rides his own head.* i. e. He takes his own precipitate courſe; like an unmanaged horſe, that ſhakes his rein in contempt of the rider. Or, to the impetuous courſe of a river, when the waters ſwell to ſuch a degree, as to break down all the banks that are raiſed to ſtop their progreſs.

. Ib. *Robes of ſable.* Arab. *a ſable ſquare veſt*, adorned with a rich double border or fringe.

Ib. *In hopes*, &c. Arab. with a deſire to enjoy a life of more eaſe and advantage: or, more literally, to grace my table with diſhes of a more delicate kind: to entertain my ſelf with ſuch repaſts as are made of dates and butter.

Ib. *Vileſt treaſure.* Arab. The very worſt ſpecies of dates, that have no kernel, and dry away ſo as not to come to maturity. The word too intimates *an hungry thief*, who ſteals any thing he can lay hold of, though of never ſo ſmall a value. He is ſo ravenous, the ſcholiaſt ſaith, as to deſpiſe nothing.

Pag. 8. *I took: origo.* I gained my point by clandeſtine windings and turnings, *Ar'wago*, &c. *more cunning* than the fox, is an Arab. proverb.

Ib. *The refuſe: al-kaṅitz wal-kaṅtzab:* the wild

beaſt

beaſt *male and female*. Proverbially applied both to fiſh-
ing and hunting. *i. e.* I ſeized the prey, great or
little, good or bad. From hence, as *Schultens* obſerves,
is explained that paſſage in *Iſai.* iii. 1. The Lord
doth take away *maſhen u-maſhenah: the ſtay and the
ſtaff:* literally, *the male and female ſtay.* i. e. the ſtrong
and weak, the great and ſmall.

Ib. *Tremble.* Arab. Nor did my ſhoulder-blade
make any trembling motion. *The muſcles of his
ſhoulder-blade trembled,* or *thundered :* or, *the ſpace
between his ſhoulders ſhook,* are phraſes with the Arabians, to ſignify a perſon's great fear.

Ib. *Divert me,* &c. There is a peculiar elegancy in
the Arabic. viz. *Did not compel me to drink at that
watering-place, which would have ſtained my honour.
Watering-place:* máwridon from wárada, *to deſcend,*
or, *go into the water ;* is here, as *Schultens* obſerves,
an emblem of *a ſplendid fortune ;* or, of *a rich man ;*
to whom people deſcend, make their addreſſes, *to
quench their thirſt:* i. e. To ſupply their neceſſities.

Ib. *Serugium,* a town in *Meſopotamia,* enriched, in it's
flouriſhing ſtate, with gardens of moſt excellent fruits,
&c. *Hariri* thus deſcribes *Serugium,* his native place,

> *My native ſoil's Serugium,*
>   *Where flows the ſtream of happineſs.*
> *The produce there of high eſteem :*
>   *The mart of plenty juſtly nam'd.*
> *The waters exquiſitely ſweet :*
>   *Like thoſe that ſpring from paradiſe.*
> *The deſerts to the eye appear,*
>   *Like verdant meadows beautiful.*
> *Th' inhabitants and houſes ſhine,*
>   *Like ſtars and ſtarry manſions bright.*
> *The air they breath delicious ſmells :*
>   *The proſpect pleaſing, large and wide.*
> *The higheſt hills are ſtrew'd with flow'rs,*
>   *When once the ſun diſſolves the ſnow.*
> *Viſit Serugium — you'll ſee*
>   *The ſeat of this world's paradiſe.*

Vid. *Schultens Indic. Geograph.* in vit. *Saladin.* Et
Origines Hebr. Tom. I. p. 301.

B   AS-

ASSEMBLY II.

ENTITLED

HULWANENSIS.

HARITH the son of *Hemmam* hath transmitted
to us what passed at the following Assembly.

From the time of my *arriving at man's estate*, and
leaving off those distinguishing *ornaments* of childhood
and youth, I have made it the business and employment of life to *frequent* such *places* as are *dedicated* to
the use of study and good learning. This course hath
engaged my earnest and intense application to such a
degree, as to carry me through tracts of land so large
and distant from each other, that even my camels,
though inured to long and tedious travels, have been
emaciated, and complained of the fatigue. The
principal reason that induced me to take this resolu-
tion, was, that wherever I happened to sojourn, I
might from thence *reap* some advantage, and collect
such materials as would be esteemed curious and entertaining: and afford as much pleasure and satisfaction, *as a cloud* does refreshment, when for a long
while we have been exposed to violent scorching heat.
So strong, even to excess, was my desire of *accomplishing this great end*, that the regularity of my
thoughts was thrown into confusion; like a series of
well-placed jewels, when once moved from their
exact conformity to each other. The measures I
pursued were as hasty, as if I was *borrowing fire* for
some immediate use, and afraid of it's being extinguished before I could have the benefit of it. The
height of my ambition was to appear in public in a
proper

proper and becoming *habit*. For which purpofe I
omitted no opportunity of converfing with men of
all degrees, from the higheft to the loweft ftation, in
hopes of *receiving inftruction* from thofe of inferior
underftanding, as well as thofe of the moft enlarged
faculties : in this manner did I folace myfelf with
the pleafing expectations of proficiency and improvement. But when I had travelled as far as *Hulwane*, and
by experience and obfervation found perfons with
whom I might be familiar, and treat them as friends
or brothers ; having made an eftimate of their good
qualities, with the fame care that one would take in
probing the depth of a wound; (knowing very well
what in the event might advance my honour; and
on the contrary, what ignominy I fhould draw on
myfelf by any difhonourable proceeding) it was my
good fortune there to meet with *Abuzeid* of *Serugium*, a man of large and extenfive *knowledge*; particularly of the diftinct branches of families who had
fignalized themfelves by any remarkable atchieve-
ments; thefe he would delineate, and trace every
ftep, every degree of advancement from their firft
original : and fo *indefatigable* in the purfuit of riches,
that he triumphed in his uncommon fuccefs : fo various and changeable in the accounts he gave of himfelf, of his birth and pedigree; that fometimes you
would hear him boaft of being defcended from the
family of *Safanidæ*, fometimes he would carry his
original as high as the princes of *Gaffan*. That he
might be particularly diftinguifhed, to day he would
appear clothed in the *habit of poets*, with a ftrait,
clofe veft: to-morrow you would fee him fhine in
the glittering ornaments of the higheft quality. But
one thing very remarkable, was, That with all this
laboured craft and artifice *to difguife* and conceal his
perfon, there was fomething in his countenance extremely pleafing; fomething in his difcourfe that
fhewed him to be a man verfed in the depths of learning; and an adept in every branch of fcience : in eloquence copious and fluent, like the rapid ftream of a

river,

river, with fo much ftrength and energy, that he
would raife in the audience not only admiration, but
in fome degree, horror and aftonifhment: and yet
with fuch eafe to himfelf, and fuch an abfolute command of fpeech, that his thoughts, though unpremeditated, were delivered in the moft beautiful expreffions of tendernefs and humanity : in fhort, a man
of thofe fuperior abilities, that the regular progrefs
he had made in arriving at the perfection of knowledge, might be compared to the fteps which gradually raife you from the loweft fituation to that of the
higheft mountains. The great advantage he received
from his extraordinary qualities was this: They
ferved him as inftruments to draw a veil over real
imperfections; fo artfully did he conceal them, and
fo little were they taken notice of, that his general
character as a man of extenfive literature, made people eagerly defirous of having even a fight of him, and
applaud themfelves when they could obtain it. So
entertaining and fo fmooth his eloquent tongue! that
every body rejoiced in his acquaintance : — and
fo *pleafant* and agreeable in his converfation! that
what requeft foever he thought proper to make, he
was fure to be gratified to the utmoft of his defire.
No wonder then that I endeavoured to *approach* as
near as poffible, when I perceived he was a perfon of
fuch peculiar properties; in his whole behaviour fo
graceful and elegant : thefe valuable accomplifhments were reafon fufficient to me why I fhould be
ambitious of his intimate friendfhip. No fooner was I
admitted to a familiarity with him, but my anxious
cares were all removed.

Time that had contracted her forehead, and affumed a difagreeable afpect, prefented herfelf with a
fmooth, chearful countenance : giving me as much
pleafure as a bridegroom receives from the fmiles and
beauteous charms of his bride. The tender refpect
with which he treated me, was fuch, that had he been
joined to me in family-alliance, his behaviour could
not have appeared in a more obliging manner. The
manfion

manſion I enjoyed, though his peculiar property, I had a full and uninterrupted poſſeſſion of. The very ſight of him was to me ſo grateful, that I may compare it to a clear fountain flowing with abundance of water; and his honourable, graceful face ſhined on me with the ſame winning air that you obſerve in a perſon when he *ſalutes* you with the ſincereſt wiſhes for your happineſs and proſperity.

In this ſituation we were placed for ſome conſiderable time: a ſituation ſo happy as to produce in me every day new and inexpreſſible delight; and to diſpel from my heart the darkeſt clouds of whatever ſeemed doubtful and obſcure. This was my happineſs till *poverty* forcing her way, gave him uneaſineſs, and was the occaſion of diſagreement and much contention : this unforeſeen change compelled him to take his leave of *Chaldea*, eſpecially when he found the *ſupplies* for preſent ſubſiſtence begin to fail him. And ſo urgent was his diſtreſs, for want of the neceſſary conveniences of life, that he was obliged to paſs through ſeveral parts of the world, in hopes of meeting with ſome place of refuge and ſafety ; till at laſt his *indigent circumſtances* brought him to a large ſociety of travellers. From this time his reſolution to purſue his intended journey grew ſo ſtrong that he made all the haſte he poſſibly could to accompliſh it. But ſo cloſely *attached* to him were his old companions, that notwithſtanding the great diſtance he was from them, their tendereſt affections for his ſafety were ſo prevalent, that they could not be ſeparated from him. When I was deprived of my friend's happy converſation, there were ſeveral who ſeemed deſirous of my familiar acquaintance, but not one did I find agreeable to me ; not one that I could have ſuch an affection for as to make myſelf intimate with him ; the reaſon was this, Since his departure there did not appear to me a ſingle perſon equal to him, in thoſe excellent and virtuous qualities, by which nature had diſtinguiſhed him to a very high degree. During this interval, which indeed was long and tedious, that he was removed

moved from me, I had no more appearance of him
than of the moon, or of a ftar, when fet in the thickeft cloud.   There was no poffibility of making any
difcovery to what part of the world he had with-
drawn himfelf : and befides, the danger attending it
might have been as great as if I had attempted to
enter into an inacceffible den of lions, or any other
retirement where immediate death was threatened ;
in fhort, there was not a man who was able to give
me the leaft intelligence of him.   Preffed with thefe
difficulties, inftead of making any farther progrefs,
I returned again to *my family* and kindred.   I then
made my appearance at *the place* he had appointed
for hearing and receiving public inftruction.

This is a Convocation or Affembly of men who
fignalize themfelves for their humanity and the improvement they make in all kinds of polite learning ;
the refort, common both to natives and foreigners.
The fociety, as ufual, being met together, a certain perfon with a thick, long beard, and a thread-bare ragged garment, prefented himfelf and made one of the
number : after he had with great civility paid his
refpects to the company that was fitting, he took his
feat in the loweft place, and foon *begun* to give them
a fpecimen of his genius, by fhewing how great a
proficient he was in learning and eloquence.   So affecting was his fubject, and fo nervous and ftrong
his *manner of fpeaking*, that every one prefent was
raifed to the higheft degree of admiration.   The perfon who fat next him taking notice of a book which
he held in his hand, had the curiofity to afk him,
what book it was ? to which he anfwered, *Abi Ibad's
Diwân:* a book univerfally efteemed for it's peculiar
excellencies.   Another queftion he put to him, *viz.*
Doft thou meet with any of thofe fubjects, to which
thine eye with curfory view feems directed, as if in
thy judgement they contained fomething worthy of
applaufe and admiration, fomething witty and facetious ? Yes, fir, he replied : I am much pleafed with
the poet's thought in the defcription he gives of an
                                              eafy,

eafy, agreeable countenance, *viz.*

> *Enrich'd with beauteous ornaments*
> *Are all the* *fmiles.* *'Tis then you fee*
> *The teeth, as cleareft iv'ry, white;*
> ' *Like pearls exact in order placed:*
> *Cool as* the berry of a cloud :
> *Sweet as the flow'rs of camomile.*

Comparifons, in my opinion, extremely fine and elegant. But he who had afked him thofe queftions, inftead of fhewing his approbation, thought he exceeded the bounds of common and intelligible language; as if his ftudied flights were too full of wonder, and deftitute of that humane and eafy manner which is requifite in all kinds of inftruction. To my apprehenfion, he faid, the fenfe of what thou deliver-eft as *found* and perfect, is really not fo; but on the contrary, difordered and imperfect, and that which thou art perfuaded *merits* large encomiums, is not indeed worthy of them. How low and inferior are thy thoughts in comparifon with thefe *verfes*, which difcover the poet's uncommon genius in the fimilies that he ufes to defcribe the beauties of teeth. *viz.*

> *So clear and white is ev'ry tooth,*
> *So clofe the union, fo compact ;*
> *That* life *without this ornament*
> *Would not afford me half it's joy.*

> *The moifture that diftils from thence,*
> *Like water in the limpid ftream,*
> *Is always frefh, is always bright,*
> *Difcolour'd with no fordid ftains.*
> *Perfection to the laft degree !*

> *Soon as the pleafing fmiles appear,*
> *You fee the beauteous iv'ry row*
> *Shine like a pearl clear from it's fhell :*
> *Not fullied with the fcorching fun,*
> *Cool and refplendent as the hail.*

> *Sweet as the flow'rs of camomile,*
> *Or thofe of palms delicious fcent,*

When

When th' ambient air is all perfume.
Like water-bubbles rising high
When mix'd with wine of gen'rous taste;
But in th' exactest order plac'd.

These verses were so entertaining, that every one there present expressed his approbation of them: so sweet and harmonious, that they commended them to the highest degree; requesting very earnestly that he would not only repeat them, but that they might have the pleasure of seeing them in writing. Another favour they desired, that he would please to inform them who was the author of those verses, and whether he was living or dead. To which he answered: *I solemnly protest* to you, that truth in my opinion appears in the most agreeable light when you do not in the least deviate from it; and I am fully persuaded, *that* veracity is most excellent, to which one pays a strict obedience: to speak freely with you, my friends, the author of those verses is the person who this day hath joined himself to you as your companion. But this manner of boasting, instead of giving satisfaction, made the company suspend their opinion: they could not persuade themselves to think he was really sincere in what he attested with so great an assurance. But he was quickly sensible, yet with some uneasiness, what it was their thoughts suggested to them; and though they endeavoured to conceal it, he thoroughly understood their intention, which was no less than an absolute denial and disproof of what he had alledged. Therefore being very apprehensive he should undergo their hasty censure and judgement, he repeated a sentence from the *Coran*, viz. *Some suspicions are criminal.* He then said, You who are critics in poetry, and such *masters* of eloquence, as to reduce it to purity and perfection, must not be displeased if I assure you that, *The true way to know whether any metal be genuine, is, to melt it down.* And if you would *examine* what is real truth, every impediment you find in this scrutiny must be entirely removed. There is another
                                                    observation

obfervation which antiquity hath obliged us with, viz. *To diftinguifh the man of honour from one of bafe principles, you muft have trial of both.* And now that I might give you full fatisfaction, I have fhewn my fecret treafures; and like the common trader who expofes his goods to fale, opened my parcel for a fpecimen of what it contains. To this, one of the perfons who ftood near, interrupting him, replied: affure yourfelf that the verfes you have repeated are very ingenious, and of an *admirable compofition:* flowing with fuch a vein of poetry, as not to admit a parallel. And this puts me upon making a farther requeft; if your poetical genius can furnifh you with fuch thoughts as will have an immediate influence upon the heart; *be fo good* as to favour us with a tafte of that nature.

To this petition he replied:

> *Behold the beauteous object's eyes!*
> *How languifhing is ev'ry change!*
> *How like* Narciffus' *flow'rs they fhine!*
> *The tears that fall, as clear as gems*
> *Frefh polifh'd from the artift's hand,*
> *Moiften the rofy-colour'd cheek.*
> *Her fingers in th' extremities*
> *Tinctur'd with red of deepeft dye:*
> *When once expos'd to common view,*
> *You're pleafed to fee the iv'ry row.*

So quick were his thoughts, that in the twinkling of an eye, or rather in lefs time, he continued his fubject in the fame agreeable manner.

> *At her approaching graceful mien,*
> *I bow'd with reverence profound,*
> *In hopes fhe'd favour my requeft*
> *To move her fcarlet-flowing veil,*
> *And entertain my lift'ning ear*
> *With founds of her harmonious voice.*
>
> *My free petition was indulg'd.*
> *The* veil *that on her beauteous face*

Brought

Brought darkness, quickly difappear'd.
Soon as we faw and heard her fpeak,
The air was fill'd with fragrant fmells
That iffued from her tender lips;
And the bright jewels all difplay'd.

They were all greatly aftonifhed at his ready faculty of delivering fuch unpremeditated thoughts; and formed to themfelves very different fentiments from what they had conceived of him; as if he was no better than a common plagiary; now freely acknowledging that the purity and fublimity of his expreffion was far removed even from the fufpicion of theft. As foon he perceived this change, and how agreeably their minds were difpofed; that fo far from having a low opinion of him, their inclination was raifed to an high degree of paying him the greateft refpect and honour imaginable; he then caft his eyes on the ground, and after a very fhort filence he refumed his poetical genius, defiring the favour of their attention; and thus proceeded:

But when the ev'ning was advanc'd,
Admonifh'd by th' approach of night ·
From focial converfe to retire;
She cloth'd herfelf in fable robes.
And like a penitent that late
Reflects on former heinous crimes;
(So ftrong th' anxiety of mind!)
Inftead of utt'ring her complaints,
On ev'ry finger took revenge.

No fooner was the veil remov'd,
The beauteous object to conceal,
But ev'ry feature difappear'd.
Nothing but fhades of darknefs feen!
Thus did the dufky robe *of night*
Obfcure Aurora's fpendid face.
Both thefe adorn'd the tender branch,
Which fhe fuftain'd with graceful air:
But ftill her reftlefs thoughts increas'd:
Of felf-compaffion void fhe rag'd,

Im-

Impreffion$ ftrong her fingers felt,
No lefs than deep and dang'rous wounds.

The applaufe was then fo general, that every fingle perfon could not but extol to the higheft degree
the real eftimate of fuch a man, and *commended the*
eloquence which he delivered with fo much eafe and
fluency. They treated him in the genteeleft and
moft *friendly manner*, and *prefented* him with a very
handfome new garment. The perfon who obliged
us with this narrative, to what he had already mentioned, adds, When I perceived the *acutenefs* of his
genius, and how remarkable were his fuperior abilities, I could not avoid looking on his countenance
with more eagernefs than I had yet done, and *indulging*
mine eye with the pleafure of making obfervations on
every mark and character: I then foon fatisfied myfelf, the perfon I was converfing with was our old
gentleman of *Serugium*; whofe long abfence from the
time I had feen him made fuch an alteration, that
the hairs of his head which before were youthful and
black, were now turned to an aged bright colour.
The pleafure that I had in congratulating my old
acquaintance, and the renewal of his entertaining
converfation was fuch, that I immediately made my
approach to pay him the utmoft veneration that was
poffible, by faluting his hand. The firft queftion
I afked him was, To what caufe muft I impute it
that there is fo great a change in your fhape, your
air, and every part belonging to you ? fo great, that
I look upon you in no other view than as an entire
ftranger; and what is it, I fhould be glad to know,
that hath occafioned fuch an alteration in your face?
your beard is as white as fnow, — fo far from being
the fame man in appearance, there is not fo much as
one outward vifible mark that makes the difcovery.
The reply that he made to him was in thefe following lines.

As water flows with limpid ftream,
Clear-iffuing from the pureft fpring,

From

From turbid, filthy mixture free;
So did my countenance appear;
And as the water-surface smooth.
But the anxieties of life,
Like an impetuous current strong
In quick succession, have defac'd
The features of my vig'rous youth.
Thus from experience we learn
With what an arbitrary hand
Fortune can rule the sons of men.

II.

How various ev'ry step she takes!
To-day like an obsequious slave
She bends her neck and crouches low;
Flatters with all her fawning smiles,
Grants ev'ry favour you request.
But mark the unexpected change!
To-morrow is a different scene.
Like an insulting conqueror,
She shakes the sword of victory:
And ravaging with tyrant-pride,
Defeats your hopes, your substance spoils.

III.

Whenev'r the earth is parch'd with drought,
Spread round with scorching, barren sands;
Should you perceive one dusky cloud,
You look for kind-refreshing show'rs.
But if the air grows bright and clear,
Your wish'd-for prospect disappears.
Such are the common treach'rous arts,
By fortune practic'd to deceive
Th' ambitious, thoughtless race of men.
The objects which she represents,
Are form'd to sooth and please the eye;
But captivate th' unguarded heart.

IV.

The best and surest remedy
To soften those perplexing thoughts

That interrupt the solid peace,
On which our happiness depends;
Is, to be resolutely brave,
And bear with patience ev'ry change.
For let calamities *severe*
Assault us like those beasts of prey,
That raven fierce, and thirst for blood:
Servile complaints a gen'rous soul
With scorn disdains; of freedom boasts,
Tho' lab'ring under heavy yokes.

V.

Would you the real virtues know,
Those ornaments that grace the man
Of truest honour, dignity,
Believe not outward pomp and shew;
Despising popular applause,
From facts alone conviction take.
Ev'n gold itself shall to the eye
Appear with all the common marks
Refin'd and pure, and yet if tried,
Prove false, adulterated coin.
But if 'tis right and genuine ore,
'Twill bear th' exactest scrutiny;
The fiery trial not refuse.
So by severe experiments
Let virtuous qualities be prov'd,
Their worth intrinsic, brighter grows.

After he had repeated these verses he rose up, and left the place; but the audience instead of being alienated and averse to him, as they had lately been, were now of a different opinion, and their affections towards him so warm, that he *drew* even *their hearts* after him.

NOTES

N O T E S

O N

A S S E M B L Y II.

ENTITLED

H U L W A N E N S I S.

P AG. 18. *Arriving at man's eftate.* Arab. *Putting on the turban.*

Ib. *Ornaments. Amulets,* or *charms:* fuch as · were faftened to children's necks to avert any mifchief, or bad accident that might happen to them. Thefe were prohibited by *Mahomet* as tokens of fuperfti-tion; and inftead of them he recommended the ufe of thefe words when danger was apprehended, viz. *maádha-'lláhi: God preferve me!* The fcholiaft on *Harîri*'s text writes, *When among the Arabians a boy arrives at a proper age, his amulets are taken from his neck, and he is adorned with a turban and a girdle, and wears a fword hanging from his neck.* Thofe amulets in fome meafure refembled the Roman *bullæ,* which the youth wore till the age of fixteen. Then, *Bulla Laribus donata pependit. Perf. Sat. v. 31.*

Ib. *Frequent — places — dedicated:* Arab. as a ftran-ger I might enter unexpectedly into the glad manfi-ons of humanity and liberal inftruction.

Ib. *Reap,* &c. The Arabic intimates, That I might hang as it were on the top of a tree, and crop from thence the choiceft fruits.

Ib. *As a cloud,* &c. In the fame figure the prophet *Ifaiah* xxv. 5. difplays the goodnefs of the Almighty in
time

time of diftrefs; *viz. Thou shalt bring down the heat with the shadow of a cloud.*

Ib. *Accomplishing*, &c. Arab. *Of kindling and spreading this fire :* viz. this eager defire of acquiring knowledge.

Ib. *Borrowing fire. To kindle his fire in hafte,* is an *Arab.* Proverb, fignifying one who takes no pains in learning, or acquiring that which is good, when both time and patience are requifite to accomplifh it. In general, he who difcharges any office in a flight, carelefs manner. Vid. *Golij Adag.* 77.

Pag. 19. *Proper habit :* to be adorned with every accomplifhment of fcience.

Ib. *Receiving inftruction*, &c. Inftead of which the Arabic expreffes his defire of being *moiftened by a large fhower of rain, and by the dew arifing from it.*

Ib. *Solace*, &c. Which the fcholiaft interprets, *I removed*, or quenched, *the thirft of my care with defire and hope.*

Ib. *Hulwane :* a town in *Affyria*, diftant about fix or feven days journey from *Bagdad.*

Ib. *Abuzeid :* diftinguifhed by the titles of the *Lamp of ftrangers*, and *Crown of the learned.* Vid. Conclufion of *Affembly* I.

Ib. *Knowledge*, &c. The Arabic intimates his fuperior talent in underftanding the forms of genealogy, in feparating one branch from another till the fpring from whence flowed the ftream of honour was difcovered. His intenfe application to this purpofe being, it feems, like the wind, which by inceffant motion blows away and difperfes fand and gravel from precious ftones, which for a long time had been concealed. The text is likewife of fo enlarged a fenfe as to fuggeft that *Abuzeid's* application to true knowledge might be compared to that of a banker, or exchanger of money, who carefully handles and examines the coin, to be fatisfied of it's intrinfic value. And to thofe artificers, whofe employment it is to melt down metals, and to make them fit and proper for the ufe they are intended.

Ib.

Ib. *Indefatigable*, &c. The Arab. phrafe, is, *To acquire riches, he fhook the earth with his foot :* intimating that his motions were as precipitate as thofe of a blind camel. that travels forward without any apprehenfion of danger.

Ib. *Safanidæ*, the fourth *Dynafty* of the kings of *Perfia* was diftinguifhed by this title ; defcended from *Safan*, whofe fon *Ardfchyr Babechan* was the founder of that empire. Vid. *Schickard Tarich. Reg. Perf.* p. 106, 107. and *Herbelot. Biblioth. Orient.* in *Saffan.*

Ib. *Gaffan.* A tribe in *Arabia Felix*, defcended from the *Afdenfes*, but compelled by an inundation to leave their native country, and fettle near a water in *Syria*, called *Gaffan*; from whence they took their name. Vid. *Pocock.* not. in *Ab. Far. Specimen Hiftor. Arab.* p. 75.

Ib. *Habit : fhiár :* a military veft, or certain mark of diftinction to know one foldier from another. The word expreffes likewife an *inward veft*, in oppofition to *dithar, the outward one*, there is a tradition of what *Mahomet* ufed to fay when he expreffed the particular regard he had for the inhabitants of *Medina* ; viz. that *they were his inner garment :* other men, *his outward one*, intimating that thofe where his true friends and affiftants. In the fame phrafe *Tamerlane* addreffes the foldiers of *Bajazet*, to perfuade them to revolt: viz. " You are the ftock of my ftocks, the branch of my branches, the member of my members. *You are to me fhiár, the inward garment.* Hift. *Tamerlane* Arab. p. 242." *Poets :* called by the Arabians *fhoaráon :* from *fhaar, to know*, or *underftand.* The reafon they give, is, becaufe the *inward, ftudious thoughts* of their minds may be compared to the military *inward garments*, which ftick clofe to the body.

Ib. *To difguife. Teláwwana : coloribus variare.* Expreffes both an inward change of mind, and an outward appearance. It is applied to one of an unfteddy temper. Such a perfon, in the Arab. *proverb, telawana, changes his colour* like the *Camelion.* This was the character of *Alcibiades*, viz. χαμαιλέοντος εὐμετάβοταβολώτερος· *more changeable than the Cameleon.* Vid. *Bochart Hieroz.* p. 1. col. 1082.

Pag. 20. *Entertaining.* Arab. *His cheek,* (or appearance) was so bewitching, that there was no turning from him without much reluctance. *Powerful in cheek,* and *powerful in language,* are promiscuous phrases among the Arabians.

Ib. *Pleasant,* &c. Arab. *The sweetness of his watering* was such, that he was able to promote an affair of any consequence.—*Watering,* with the Arabians, carries the same meaning as *agreeable conversation:* and *warada, to descend,* is equivalent to *going into the water.*—As in the Arab. *Proverb,* " I will not do it till the *land-crocodile yarido, descends:*" *(goes into the water.)* i. e. I will never do it. Vid. *Bochart Hieroz.* p. 1. lib. 4. col. 1047.'—*Schultens* observes, we have the same idiom in *Isai.* lxiii. 14. viz. As a beast, *tered, goeth down* into the valley : viz. to *drink* and refresh himself.

Ib. *Approach,* &c. Arab. *To hang upon the borders of his garment.* A figurative way of speaking among the Arabians, intimating the eager desire of enjoying any one's society and friendship.—*To stick close to the loose fringe of protection or patronage,* is in the east a character of *clients* and *dependants.*—Comp. *Zech.* viii. 23. Ten men—shall *take hold of the skirt* of a Jew.

Ib. *Ambitious.* Arab. *Aspire,* or *pant after.*

Pag. 21. *Salutes,* &c. Arab. *when he wishes you plenty of rain, and plenty of provision.* Or, according to a known phrase of the Arabians, when he salutes you with this friendly salutation : viz. *God bless your countenance.* Comp. *Numb.* vi. 25. The Lord *make his face shine upon thee!* Ps. xxxi. 16.

Ib. *Poverty,* &c. The full sense of the Arabic is, *till the hand of poverty mingled for him the cup of strife and division ; as the apothecary and surgeon with proper instruments mix and prepare medicines and salves for their patients.*—By *the cup,* good or evil is expressed in scripture : viz. *the cup of salvation,* and *the*

C   *cup*

cup of fury, trembling and astonishment : Psal. cxvi. 13.
Isai. li. 17. Ezek. xxiii. 33:—Expressions of the same
kind are familiar to the Arabians. The author of
Tamerlane, in his sublime style, speaking of the enemy's defeat, writes; p. 228. *They made every man
drink two cups ; one of death, the other of poverty*: i. e.
They took away both their life and substance.—And
in terms yet stronger, p. 322. *Behold the butler of
death, who oppressed them with cups of destruction.—
Cups mixed with tempests*, are mentioned, p. 320, viz.
*They gave them to drink a cup of tempest by day, and a cup
of tempest by night*. Comp. Psal. xi. 6.   Upon the
wicked he shall rain snares; fire and brimstone, and
an horrible tempest—the portion of their cup.

Ib. *Supplies*, &c. literally, *The want of a bone to
gnaw urged him to bid farewel* [to divorce himself
from] *to Chaldea.*—The comparison is made with regard to an hungry dog, which leaves the bone when
he can get no more flesh from it : and to a man di-
vorced from his wife ; without the least thoughts of
returning to her again.

Ib. *Indigent*, &c. Arab. *The trembling vibration
of the standard of poverty joined him to the company* (or
thread) *of associated travellers* :—intimating not only
the uneasiness which poverty frequently occasions ;
but the series or order of the eastern way of travelling,
when the Arabians, like camels in the wilderness,.
move one after another so close as if they were joined
together by a line or thread : [the camel's nose that
follows being fastened to the tail of that which goes
before.]   From hence it is that the Arabians say, *we
have threaded the way*, i. e. we proceeded in a long
straight line.   *Standard of poverty*: i. e. Such as is
visible and conspicuous.   *Standard: ráyaton*: a word
applied by the Arabians to *good*, or *bad fortune* : which
they express by *a white or black standard*.   Amongst
other significations it particularly denotes *a military
standard* ; from the radix, *to see*: being erected so as
to appear to the whole army.   And from it's *trembling
vibration* when displayed, it expresses that *terror*, or
dread,

dread, which arifes from any fudden difappointment of our ftrongeft hopes.

Ib. *Attached,* &c. Arab. *When he took his leave their hearts followed him* [*bi-azimmátihi*] *in his head-ftalls;* i. e. as the fcholiaft explains it, *The hearts of his companions were joined as clofe to him as a cord with a ring is joined to a camel's nofe,* that the traveller may with more eafe guide and direct him. A metaphor frequently ufed by the Arabs : viz. " He put *zimá-man, the headftall* of the bufinefs into his hand." *Hift. Tamerl.* p. 343. i. e. he committed the whole affair to his management. *To let go,* or *loofe the headftall,* is a phrafe of the fame force; viz. to entruft another with your concerns. From hence we muft approve of *Schultens's* correction of *Pfal.* cxl. 9. where inftead of rendering *zemamo al tapek, further not his wicked device :* we fhould rather fay, *capiftrum ejus ne finas exire : fuffer not his headftall to be loofe;* i. e. give him not too much liberty. The confequence then will be juft : *let not thofe who compafs me about exalt themfelves!* according to bifhop *Hare's* tranflation. The 17th *Pfalm* ℣. 3. will admit of the fame conftruction : not, *I am purpofed* that *my mouth fhall not tranfgrefs:* but *zammóthi, capiftro alligavi,* ne tranfgrediatur os meum. *I have bri-dled,* or *laid a reftraint on* my mouth left it fhould tranfgrefs.

Pag. 22. *To my family,* &c. Arab. *To the fpreading of my branch.* i. e. To my kindred and relations. Comp. *Job* xv. 33. The flame fhall dry up *his branches. John* xv. 5. I am the vine, ye are *the branches.*

Ib. *The place,* &c. Arab. *The houfe, or manfion of his books.*

Ib. *Begun,* &c. *to produce his bottles of milk.* Every thing of value and of high efteem among the Arabians, is diftinguifhed by *milk. How large his flow of milk!* is the fame with them as, *how learned, how copious, how eloquent !* there is another interpretation of *bottles,* but not fo applicable to our author's intention : as if by a *bottle* was meant the *body,*

C 2 which

·which is a veffel for the foul. From hence it is fa'd of a perfon that dies, or is killed, his *bottle is empty.*

Ib. *Manner of speaking :* Arab. *The diftinction of his speech.* Such, the commentator obferves, as is plain and intelligible to the auditors. Such as, *Mahomet* faith, God gave to *David. Alcor.* ch. 38. 21.

Ib. *Diwán :* a *regifter,* a lift of names civil or military. Any compofition, efpecially *poetical.* From the fame radix, *To judge,* the fupreme council or fenate of the Turks is named *diwán. Abu Ibad,* commonly called *Bochteri,* was a celebrated poet. vid. *Herbelot.*

Pag. 23. *The berry of a cloud.* i. e. *The hail.*

Ib. *Sound,* &c. Arab. That which thou thinkeft is fat and flourifhing, is attended with fome morbific tumour.

Ib. *Merits,* &c. Arab. *Thou blowest that thou may'ft raife fire, where there is no fuel to kindle it.* Agreeable to which is the cenfure of an Arab. poet reflecting on a perfon who labours to finifh any kind of work without proper materials, *viz.*

> *The fire by blowing may be rais'd :*
> *But if the afhes once be dead,*
> *To blow is labour fpent in vain.*

Ib. *Verfes : Houfes.* From the form of a tent, and the parts belonging to it the Arabians take the words of their profody. As tents have *ftakes* and *cords* to keep them firm; fo is a verfe fecured by *feet,* diftinguifhed by the names of *ftakes* and *cords.* The *ftake* confifting of three letters; the *cord* only of two. By the fame metaphor an hemiftic, or half-verfe, is called *one part of a folding door.* vid. *Sam. Cleric. Tract.* de *Profodia Arabica.*

Ib. *Life,* &c. The literal verfion is, *Let my life be a facrifice for my teeth that fhine with the brighteft fplendour!* Intimating, he had rather lofe his life than his teeth. This extravagant way of *devoting* is common to the Arabians. For inftance: *Let my father be made a facrifice for thee!* as if he had faid; *Thy* life is more precious to me than even my father's.

ther's. *Let my family and kindred be his redemption!* i. e. To me he is dearer than all my friends.

Ib. *Perfection: nahiyaca.* A word used to express *sufficiency*, or whatever is perfect either in things or persons. This man, or this woman *nahiyaca, sufficit tibi.* i. e. *is of so great advantage to thee as to excel all others.*

Pag. 24. *Water-bubbles: hebeb.* A word of an enlarged sense, denoting *a berry, a regular set of teeth,* and *bubbles,* which like a *series of berries* rise on the surface of wine when mixed with water.

— Ib. *I solemnly protest: aimo-'llábi:* for *aimono: per Deum,* literally, *dextra Dei;* a common form of an oath among the Arabians. *Lifting up the hand,* in Scripture, is the same with *swearing:* as *Gen.* xiv. 22. *I have lift up my hand.* i. e. I have sworn. *Exod.* vi. 8. *Num.* xiv. 30.

Ib. *Coran: al-cor.* ch. 49. 12. we read, " O ye believers, be very much upon your guard as to suspicion: because some suspicions are criminal. To which *Mahomet* adds, *neither be ye curious in examining other people's concerns; nor do one of you reflect on another in his absence.* To discourage them from such practices he puts this important question: *what! would any of you desire to eat the flesh of his dead brother? surely you would abhor it.* The Apostle speaks the same language in his *Ep.* to the *Galat.* v. 15. *If ye bite and devour one another, take heed that ye be not consumed one of another.*

Ib. *Masters,* &c. Arab. Physicians or surgeons to vitious and diseased language.

Ib. *To know,* &c. A common eastern proverb, intimating that diligent enquiry is the only way to find out what is real and substantial virtue.

Ib. *Examine,* &c. Arab. *The hand of truth cuts off the garment of doubt,* from hence is that figurative expression, *God clothed him with the garment of his own work.* i. e. Rewarded him according to his merit. The word for *garment,* viz. *ridáon,* signifies *a debt.* — An Arabian physician's prescription to a man who desired long life, among other things, was, To wear

C 3 *al-*

al-ridáa, a light-garment. i. e. as it is explained, *Not to burden himself by running into debt: Abul. Pharag. Hift. Dynaft.* p. 158. The fame word is by a meta-phor applied both to *liberality* and *covetoufnefs.* A man with a deep, loofe, flowing robe is the fame with one of a generous temper. The reverfe to him is, He who appears in a fhort narrow garment.

Pag. 25. *Have trial.* Arab. You muft be as careful in clearing away all obftruc̈tions, as a man is, when he fmooths and polifhes his inftruments.

Ib. *Admirable compofition.* The literal Arabic com-pares this poetry to a piece of artificial work, fuch as was never taken from *minwálon, the weaver's beam. To weave from another man's beam,* is the fame as *fub-fcribing to his opinion.* That both good and evil were decreed by God, was the doctrine of a fect among the Arabians. *Wafil Ibn Ata,* we are told, *embraced their opinion:* literally, weaved *álai minwálihim according to their beam. Pocock.* Not. in *Ab. Far. Spec. Hift. Arab.* p. 194.

Ib. *Vein: kárichah.* Properly, the firft clear water that iffues from a new well; To this the Commenta-tor refembles *a fine genius,* from which flows good fenfe and underftanding. The verb in the eighth conjugation emphatically fignifies, *To have the vein,* or talent, *of fpeaking extempore either in verfe or profe.* In oppofition to which *a frozen* or *congealed vein* is the fame with *ignorance* and *ftupidity. Hift. Timur.* p. 30.

Ib. *Be fo good,* &c. Arab. Give us a fet of jewels placed according to that fafhion.

Ib. *Narciffus' flowers;* of a mixed-yellow colour, with which, the fcholiaft faith, are compared languifh-ing eyes. The literal tranflation of the verfes fhews the fublime of eaftern ftyle, viz. *She rains jewels from her Narciffus's.* i. e. She drops tears like jewels from her eyes, that languifh like the flowers of Narciffus. *And moiftens the rofe.* i. e. The rofy-cheek. *And bites the grapes with hail.* i. e. puts her fingers, the ex-tremities of which are dyed with a colour like that of red grapes, to her mouth, when her teeth appear as round

round and white as hail. vid. p. 37.

Pag. 40. *Harmonious voice.* Arab. The aromatics of her voice.

Pag. 25, 26. *The veil, &c. disappeared.* Arab. *She removed the redness of the twilight, which shaded the splendor of the moon.* i. e. she took off the red hood from her fair face. *Splendor : sánan.* Such as that which precedes thunder; in allusion to which the Arabian laments the loss of his sons that were killed in battle, viz. *The two luminaries of war which I had kindled were soon extinguished.* i. e. The two sons whom I had brought up and instructed in the art of war were soon destroy'd. *Whose* [*sánan*] *light'ning shined to night-travellers.* i. e. Whose courage was a protection to any one labouring under difficult circumstances.

Pag. 26. *Fragrant smells, &c.* Arab. *She let the jewels* [i. e. her precious words] *fall from her sweet-smelling seal.* i, e. her mouth, issuing out her sweet breath. Comp. *Mat.* vii. 6. where *precious words* are compared to *pearls.* The Arabian poets frequently resemble *the mouth* when shut, to a *seal* that is round and close united. In the same language the *scales* of *Leviathan* are shut up together as *a close seal. Job* xli. 15.

Ib. *On every finger, &c.* Arab. Bit the extreme parts of her fingers.

Ib. *Dusky robe, &c.* Arab. *Night appeared upon Aurora.* i. e. The black veil was thrown over her bright face.

Ib. *Tender branch.* i. e. *The young virgin,* compared for her erect stature to the branch of a tree. [In Homer's phrase, ἀνέδραμεν ἔρνεϊ ἴσον· *succrevit ramo similis. Iliad.* 18. 56.] Our poet introduces his *branch* carrying on her head both *night* and *Aurora.* The latter in her face; the former in her veil.

Pag. 27. *Impressions, &c.* Arab. *She gnawed her beryls with her radiant pearls.* i. e. She made deeper impressions than before, on her fingers, which were long and round like cylinders, with her shining teeth.

Ib. *Commended, &c.* Arab. They spake much in

C 4   praise

praife of *his gentle rain.* i. e. his eloquence that came
from him like *dimáton,* which fignifies *a filent, ftill
rain, that falls without thunder or ftorm, and continues
for two or three days.* Compare *Deut.* xxxii. 2. *My
doctrine fhall drop* as *the rain — as the fmall rain upon
the tender herb.*

Ib. *Friendly manner.* Arab. *ifhraton,* the number
Ten. i. e. in the fame manner as if he was one of the
friendly fociety of the Arabians, which ufually confifted of that number.

Ib. *Prefented, &c.* Arab. *They made his bark fhine :*
a man's clothes which cover the body, being figuratively
expreffed by bark which covers the trees.

Ib. *Acutenefs, &c.* Arab. *The pure bright flame of his
torch.*

Ib. *Remarkable, &c.* Arab. *How glittering his
fplendor.*

Ib. *Indulging, &c.* Arab. *I fuffered mine eye to take
a free repaft on the fignal marks by which he diftinguifhed himfelf.*

Ib. *The hairs, &c.* Arab. *His dark night, now
fhined with a glimmering light like that of the moon.*

Pag. 28. *Dufky cloud,* Arab. *The thundering of a
barren cloud.* A proverbial expreffion, intimating pro-
feffions of kindnefs made in ftrong terms, but in the
event deceitful. Applied to one who makes large pretences to generofity and other virtuous qualities ; but
is really deftitute of them. [vid. *Adag. Arab.* iv. Ed.
Gol. *Robba, &c. very often there is but little water
after a thundering cloud.*] A perfon of this difpofition
the Arabians fay, *lightens and thunders,* i. e. without
rain. *Clouds without rain,* is St. *Jude*'s character of
falfe teachers. y. 12. — On the contrary, one of *Nawabig*'s fentences is,

*The cloud that fends forth rain when it thunders,
Is like him who fpeaks truth when he promifes.*

When the *Sultan* of *Egypt* brought his forces into *Syria*
to oppofe *Tamerlane;* and inftead of fighting return'd
home ; the inhabitants of *Damafcus* being then in a
de-

deplorable condition ; *Arabsjades* [*Hift. Timur.* p.195.] from a certain poet writes ;

A thund'ring cloud gave hopes of fhow'rs,
To quench the army's parching thirft,
But as the ftormy wind increas'd,
They faw the flatt'ring cloud difperfe.

Pag. 29. *Calamities : al-chotówbo. Nawabig* ob-ferves ;

Sickneſs and poverty are [*al-chotobáni*] *two calamities,*
Bitterer than the juice of a wild gourd.

Ib. *Aſſault,* &c. *adra.* A word properly applied to *the miſeries of life:* intimating that they give us as much pain as if a fierce grey-hound, or a ravenous wolf fhould feize on us for their prey.

Ib. *Drew their hearts,* &c. *moſtá-ſhibon: Aſ-ſociated to himſelf* their hearts. *Sáhibon: ſocius:* is a word of great uſe among the Arabians. *The ſocius* of a country, is the fame with them as *lord* of it. *Mahomet* is diſtinguiſhed by the titles of, *The ſocius of vocation, and legation,* i.e. in their interpretation, *called* by God, and his *Ambaſſador. The ſocius of riches, of lenity, of building,* intimates one who is *wealthy.* A man *of humane diſpoſition.* An *Architect. Jonas* in the whale's belly, they call *The ſocius of a fiſh. A priſoner, the ſocius of a priſon.* A deceaſed perſon con-demned for his fins, *The ſocius of fire, and of hell.* On the contrary, *The ſocii of a garden,* are fuch as enter into an *heavenly paradiſe.* Forms of this kind are fre-quently read in the *Alcoran.* What the Arabians ex-preſs by *ſáhibon,* the Hebrews do by *Baal. Gen.* xiv. 13. *Confederates* are *Baalim, the ſocii* of a covenant. xxxvii. 19. *A dreamer, Baal, the ſocius* of dreams. xlix. 23. *Archers, Baale, ſocii* of arrows. *Exod.* xxiv. 14. He whoſe affairs require the judgement of others, is, *Baal debarim, ſocius,* vel, *poſſeſſor verborum,* vel *rerum:* hath matters of conſequence to communicate. *A bird, Prov.* i. 17. is *Baal canaph. Poſſeſſor of wing.* xxix. 22. *A furious man, Baal bhemah: poſſeſſor of fury.*

ASSEM-

ASSEMBLY III.

ENTITLED

KAILANENSIS.

THE subject of this Assembly transmitted to us by *Harith* the son of *Hemmam* is as follows. At a certain place where I *joined* myself to a small society of men, with whom I had cultivated an intimate friendship; the discourse that passed was so agreeable, and so much to the purpose, that not one person in the company spoke any thing but was *approved of*; answering in all respects the expectations which had possessed my thoughts before the time appointed came for our assembling together. To what shall I compare this harmony? I may resemble it to fire, which without fail kindles when you apply one proper *instrument* so as to correspond exactly with another. There was no *appearance* of strife and contention, their sentiments being so unanimous as not to admit of the least opposition. Here our custom was, *to recite* certain verses, and every one present reciprocally to take his turn, *entertaining* one another with the most elegant flowers of such poetry as our thoughts then suggested to us. Whilst our time was thus employed, of a sudden who should rise up but one that was an entire stranger to us, clothed in an old, ragged vest, deformed in his body, lame in his feet, and who addressed us in this manner: O ye best and choicest treasures, a concert of the most joyful and sweetest-sounding instruments! I wish you a happy morning, and may you *enjoy* it in the fullest and largest sense! my request to you is, that with
com-

compaſſion you would pleaſe to caſt an eye on a man,
who in his proſperity was remarkably diſtinguiſhed
and celebrated for a large and numerous *houſhold, an
unbounded generoſity*, a *plenteous ſtream* of riches, con-
veniencies and advantages of life without number;
eſtates and villages of wide extent, in a word, fur-
niſhed with every uſeful and neceſſary medium that
could be accommodated to promote hoſpitality; a-
dapted to the gracious reception of ſtrangers and
travellers. But amidſt all theſe enjoyments I was
very ſenſible that *fortune*, inſtead of that agreeable countenance which for a long time had ſmiled on
me, was ſo much changed, that I perceived nothing
but diſtaſtful frowns, wrinkles deep as furrows made
by the plough, grinding and gnaſhing of teeth. The
ſorrows that attacked me were like the wars of enemies: ſparks of envy unquenchable, of the moſt ma-
lignant ſort, were kindled againſt me. Calamities of the
moſt direful nature came upon me in very quick ſucceſ-
ſions. To ſo low a degree of poverty was I reduced,
that the hollow of my hand gave as empty a ſound as
that which echoes from an houſe deſtitute of inhabitants and ſpoiled of it's goods. Not one of thoſe numerous cattle which uſed to fill the ſpacious area were now
to be ſeen. My ſubſtance was ſo large, and my munificence in proportion to it ſo extenſive; that I might
compare them to thoſe plenteous ſtreams that flow in
ſuch abundance from inceſſant, living fountains.
But now they are quite decayed and dried up, ſub-
ſided into the earth, and no remains of the iſſue from
whence they came to be diſcovered. My *ſpring-man-
ſion* remarkable for plenty of graſs and all kinds of
uſeful herbage; and where I took the utmoſt delight,
the ſoil being plain, ſoft and commodious for the
moſt pleaſurable walks, is now ſo neglected, ſo rugged
and hard, that you would think the nature of it was
quite altered from what it appeared before. Inſtead of
numbers of men whoſe obligations for favours they
had received demanded frequent attendance; nothing
but abſence and a profound ſolitude, ſuch as one per-
ceives

ceives in deferts and void places! inftead of *beds* of the
fofteft and tendereft fafhion, prepared for the repofe
of thofe who are fatigued with the labour and heat of
the day; nothing to reft on but bare ground, *ftrewed*
with pebbles, gravel-ftones, and every thing you can
imagine that occafions pain and uneafinefs. Such is
my prefent condition; once happy and profperous;
now the very reverfe to all my former enjoyments:
The confequence of which misfortunes is this; from
chearful domeftics, who were nourifhed and fupport-
ed by me in the moft elegant, fumptuous manner,
you hear nothing but loud voices of weeping and affecting lamentation. Stables and folds, built for the
reception and clofe confinement of cattle of various
kinds, are now quite *deferted*. So deplorable my circumftances, that even the fame men who looked with
a jealous eye on my profperous condition, are now affected towards me with bowels of the tendereft compaffion. They are fenfible of my diftrefs, being deprived not only of my *cattle*, but of all that *wealth*
and fortune, which I lately poffeffed in great abundance. I am now pitied by thofe who envied me;
lamented by fuch as ufed to rejoice at other men's calamities. By the ftroke of adverfe fortune falling on
me with the utmoft violence, in an hafty, tumul-
tuous manner, bruifing and wounding me as it were
with fome heavy inftrument of cruelty; and by the
injurious affault of poverty, the whole ftrength of
my body is fo much weakened, that I am forced to
ftoop, and bow down to the earth, and to *tread the*
ground with the greateft caution for fear of ftumbling.
My prefent food, inftead of affording me good and
real nourifhment, is, every morfel I take, ready to
ftrangle me. Inftead of *alleviating* thofe inward dif-
orders, which like a continued raging heat give me
inexpreffible uneafinefs, I rather find them increafe to
a much higher degree. The want of common provifion is fo great, that my bowels, pinched with
hunger, are much contracted. When I am fatigued
with the burden of the day, and lie down in expectation

tion of taking natural reft; fo far from *folacing* myfelf with common and ordinary fleep, my thoughts
are perplexed and diffipated : a conftant. vigilance
prevents that refrefhment which I am defirous of, and
for which I labour with great anxiety. My dwelling-
place is now very different from it's ufual fituation.
I am obliged to live in low and humble *valleys*. The
ground I formerly paffed over, though *rough and
fpread with thorns*, yet was fmooth and plain in comparifon of that I now tread on. In moving from one
place to another I travelled with fo much eafe and
pleafure, that I did not fo much as think of beafts of
burden to carry me : but now fo rugged are my paths
that I am glad of any help or eafe that I can poffibly
meet with. The calamities that happened to me in
former days, though fudden and unexpe&ted, forcing
their way with impetuous violence, like that of an ir-
refiftable inundation, which eradicates, and deftroys
whatever obftru&ts it's paffage, were yet in my opinion in a great meafure tolerable, was I to compare
them with the continued, inceffant deftru&tion with
which I am now on every fide invaded. I was then
ready to think that the period of time, determined
by fate, moved with a flow pace : but now I am per-
fuaded the motion is much protra&ted. Is there not
one man to be found of fuch an ingenuous fpirit, as
to afford fome medicine or other to foften and heal
my deep wounds ? not one perfon of fo liberal and
generous a temper, as to diftinguifh himfelf by folacing me with mild and compaffionate treatment ?
to what caufe muft I afcribe my misfortunes? to him,
no doubt, from whom I am defcended: to that branch
of the family who derive their origin from *Kaila.*
That I muft efteem the principal foundation of my
poverty: the circumftances I am reduced to being fo
neceffitous, that I have not fo much as a fupply of
one night's provifion.

To this complaint *Harith* the fon of *Hemmam* replied; my affe&tion to fo miferable an obje&t of
poverty is raifed an high degree, and my inclination

tion to give him all the eafe and comfort imaginable is very ftrong and urgent; efpecially as I am
in hopes that by this means I fhall have the pleafure
of being *entertained* with fome of his elegant poetry.
I then took out for him a piece of gold; and to fatisfy my curiofity, I faid, if thou wilt favour us with a
fpecimen of thy poetical genius, in praife of this
piece; it fhall be thy own property, as fure as it can
be affigned by any court of juftice. Without farther
folicitation he immediately granted the requeft; and
in his ufual extempore way repeated the following
verfes, the fole produce of his own thoughts, and
not falfly arrogating to himfelf the compofition of
any perfon whatfoever.

I.

That piece of pureft metal,
  Of clear uncommon luftre,
With powerful attraction
  Demands my higheft praifes.
To travel is it's pleafure
  Through diff'rent, diftant countries;
Difdaining the confinement
  Of abject, fordid mifers.

II.

Thy fame is univerfal.
  In ev'ry place thy prefence
With all the marks of honour
  Is rev'renc'd and applauded.
Thy fhining face diftinguifh'd
  With lines of deep impreffion,
To ev'ry eye difcovers
  A vein of fecret treafure.

III.

Bus'nefs by thee conducted,
  Moves free and expeditious;
Like darting rays that vibrate
  From ftars in clofe conjunction.

So

So lovely are thy features,
  That ev'n the highest paffions
Submit to all thy precepts,
  As flaves to tyrant-mafters.

IV.

Thy influence fo engaging,
  As if our hearts in fubftance
Were ore of gold and filver,
  The brighteft coins producing.
Obferve the man of fortune,
  Whofe bags are full and fwelling;
How infolent his triumphs
  O'er poor inferior objects!

V.

But fhould thofe bags diminifh,
  And th' hidden ftore that languifh'd
In their ungrateful prifon,
  Break from the felfifh mafter:
How foon wilt thou recover
  Thy former bright appearance,
And raife the admiration
  Of ev'ry new fpectator!

VI.

How wilt thou gain th' affection,
  And popular applaufes
Of thofe, who with impatience
  Were waiting for thy bounty.
Concerns of greateft moment,
  Entrufted to thy province;
With what fuccefs attended,
  Wealthy acceffions teach us.

VII.

But fhould thy gracious prefence
  Retire like th' ebbing water;
Our flowing ftream of plenty
  Would quickly lofe it's currcnt.
    Prefage of anxious forrow!

Let

Let troubles rise like armies;
  Rage like the sea tempestuous;
On ev'ry side attack us!
  Thy friendly mediation,
      Those cares and storms disperses.

VIII.

But change the scene : *what troubles*
  Attend thy secret motions!
When men of bright examples
  Fall from their height of glory.
Should wrath and anger kindled,
  Break out in flames of passion;
Threat'ning some quick destruction
  To those wh' oppose thy torrent;

IX.

Thy friendly interposing,
  By softest strains of whisper,
Will soon alloy the fury
  Of the most dang'rous tempest.
What miserable objects,
  In jails and prisons tortur'd,
Betray'd by false pretenders
  To kindred and alliance,
Have chang'd their cells of darkness,
  For freedom and enlargement!

X.

Should we attempt to number
  The sev'ral institutions,
By thee our Lord and Sov'reign
  At different times created;
      The labour would be fruitless.

So sacred are thy virtues,
  Did not that lawful rev'rence
Religion claims, forbid us;
  As God we should adore thee,
      Thy golden image worship.

After

After this large encomium on the piece of gold, *Abuzeid*, in expectation of receiving it, stretched forth his hand, and said, " *A man* of ingenuous principles by some reprefentation or other shews how ready he is to perform his promife. So whenever we hear it thunder, we conclude there is fuch a difpofition in the heavens, that we shall foon fee fome plenteous showers of rain."

He then threw him the piece of money, and faid, Take it with the fame readinefs and pleafure that I give it thee : which, as foon as he received, he raifed to his mouth, expreffing himfelf in the ufual form of benediction, praying, that *God would blefs his benefactor.* After this he *gathered up* his loofe garment, and prepared to take his leave, acknowledging the favour beftowed on him in the fulleft terms of gratitude. His facetious behaviour was fo entertaining as to affect me to fome *degree of uneafinefs* ; for I begun to think that my generofity to him was inconfiderate, and rather too much contracted. And indeed before this incident I was never fo fenfible of the pain and difgrace that muft neceffarily attend thofe men whofe circumftances are fuch as oblige them to become debtors to others. Therefore without farther confideration I took out of my purfe another piece of money, and faid, Is there any reafon why thou shouldeft fpeak in difpraife of money, and after that think proper to receive it? to which, without giving himfelf the leaft time to premeditate, he raifed his voice, like one who fings when he is driving his camels ; and repeated the following lines in the fweeteft and moft delightful accents.

I.

Curfe *on the great deceiver,*
    With all his fpecious falfhood.
T' attract, t' engage th' affection,
    He shines with deepeft yellow ;
True hypocrite *in action,*
    His double front difcovers.

D   II.

II.

What sudden, quick vibrations
  Dart from these glitt'ring aspects,
To captivate th' unguarded,
  Incurious spectator!
Bright *as the beauteous object*
  Of the most am'rous passion:
But *with that sinking languish,*
  Which spreads the face of lovers.

III.

But would you ask th' opinion
  Of men of sense and judgement;
Of *simple* truth tenacious,
  Strangers to arts delusive:
They'll readily convince you,
  The anxious thoughts of misers
Provoke the great Creator,
  And call for indignation.

IV.

Was ev'ry one contented
  With providential measures;
That law of amputation
  Would never been enacted.
No injury *vexatious,*
  No violent oppression,
Would dare t' appear in publick,
  To break *the rules of justice.*

V.

No man of sordid temper,
  In near or distant climate,
Would shrink *with dread and horror,*
  To bear the voice of strangers,
In darkest nights bewilder'd;
  But give the best reception,
The kindest entertainment,
  To ev'ry weary trav'ller.

2   VI.

VI.

No creditors deluded
  By ſtratagems of debtors,
By artful means protracting
  Th' appointed days of payment.

VII.

Envy *with evil aſpect,*
  Darting her pois'nous arrows,
Would never had exiſtence.
  That common form *of refuge,*
T' avoid the ſtroke of vengeance,
  Had never been repeated.

VIII.

How ſtrangely *form'd by nature!*
  How vitiated his morals!
What qualities attend him!
  Whoſe aid when chiefly wanted,
Is uſeleſs, inſufficient
  Your anxious cares to ſoften;
Till th' happy time approaches
  Of his ſecure deliv'rance,
From an obſcure confinement:
  When free and unmoleſted,
A fugitive from bondage,
  He takes his flight as uſual,
Like quick-ſilver he paſſes
  Through paths of ſtraiteſt compaſs.

IX.

Does ſuch a crafty artiſt
  Deſerve our approbation?
So far from common merit,
  That he's to be applauded
With trueſt marks of honour,
  Who from the higheſt *mountain*
Devotes to ſure deſtruction,
  This cunning, ſervile wand'rer.

X.

X.

How excellent his temper!
How firm his refolution!
Who, when addrefs'd and flatter'd
With baits of am'rous paffion,
With charms of golden afpect,
Refifts with manly courage;
Difdains a low fubmiffion
To the deceitful tempter.

XI.

In terms of th' utmoft freedom,
Such fentiments delivers,
As truth herfelf would dictate,
Was her advice requefted.
With thee I've no alliance,
No mutual converfation.
Give me no more difturbance:
Purfue thy vagrant courfes.

But to fatisfy him I was pleafed with his poetry,
I faid, how fluent and copious is thy eloquence,
which difcharges itfelf like an hafty, impetuous fhower of rain : to which, without taking any notice of
the compliment, he replied, *The condition is of weigh-*
tier moment. I then *prefented* him with the fecond
piece of gold : faying, *Secure them both with thofe*
guardian verfes of the Coran. He immediately put it
to his mouth to affociate with the other as twins.
And on his retiring from the company, he fpoke in
praife of his *morning-adventure*; expreffing in fulleft terms the fatisfaction he received from the Affembly he had happily met with, greatly applauding
their generous munificence.

From the particular manner in this, and in feveral
other circumftances, which *Harith Ibn Hemmam* had
taken notice of, he could not avoid faying, My mind
did as it were whifper and privately fuggelt to me that
this man muft furely be *Abuzeid:* and the outward
appearance of his being lame, that is one of his arti-
ces

fices to deceive us. I then defired he would not leave us, plainly telling him, it is in vain for thee to affume to thyfelf a different perfon; for thou art fufficiently difcovered by the eloquence which thou haft difplayed in fuch lively ftrong colours: therefore let me advife thee to tread the ground as ufual, with the fame fteddy upright fteps. To this he replied, if thou art *Ibn Hemmam,* my moft refpectful and honourable compliments are due to thee: and *may thy life* be preferved among thofe who are diftinguifhed by their noble birth and quality! if thou art really defirous of knowing the perfon who is now talking with thee: I am *Harith*; but let me intreat thee to give an account of thy ftate and condition: what fortune, what accidents have happened to thee? To this he made anfwer, The condition of my life hath been fuch as to pafs through great variety. My circumftances have fometimes been diftreffed and miferable: at other times I have enjoyed the good things of this world, riches and honour in abundance. I may compare myfelf to the mariner at fea; to-day he ftruggles with ftorms and tempefts: to-morrow the heavens are calm and ferene. But what reafon doft thou give for counterfeiting thyfelf lame? a pofture fo different from thy ufual appearance, and fo very difagreeable, as to make thee a jeft and ridicule to every one who fees thee. This rebuke had fuch an effect, that his countenance, which generally was eafy, chearful, compofed; bright as the moon, or a ftar, when fhining in full fplendor; immediately altered to darknefs and obfcurity, as if a thick heavy cloud was drawn over it. Then turning himfelf from the company, he repeated the following verfes:

I.

'Tis true in lamenefs I'm a counterfeit;
But not my choice: neceffity's the caufe.
By this expedient I remove thofe pains
That aggravate the poor man's great diftrefs.
Ev'n the feign'd wandring cripple's heart is glad

To

To find admittance at the rich man's gate,
And take refreshment from his bounteous hand.

II.

Happy in liberty without restraint,
Like camel feeding, not confin'd by reins,
I change the barren for a fruitful soil.
As those who halt in various sentiments
Of their religious duties, I indulge
A wanton fancy, in pursuit of ease.

III.

These principles of such unsteddy course,
No wonder if in general condemn'd!
Subjects of common popular dispraise!
But all invective satyr, pray, forbear :
The gifts of nature we must not despise.
Instructed by her in this artful way,
The privilege of blameless I demand.

NOTES

NOTES

ON

ASSEMBLY III.

ENTITLED

KAILANENSIS.

PAG. 42. *Kailanensis.* [Vid. p. 19. *Assembly* II.]
Kaila, from whom *Abuzeid* derives his pedigree,
the scholiast writes, was the mother of *Ausi* and *Char-
zebi*, the daughter of *Arkan*, of the *Gassan* family.
[Vid. p. 45.] *Golius* observes that *Aus* is the name of a
tribe in Arabia Felix, the father of which was *Aus*
the son of *Kaila*, and brother of *Alcharezji*. From
these two brothers descended the *Ansars*, or *Adjutors*,
inhabitants of *Medina*, peculiarly so called, because
above all others they were assistants to *Mahomet* in
his expeditions. This *third Assembly* takes the title
of *Kailanensis* from the above mentioned *Kaila*.

Ib. *Joined.* The Arab. verb *náduma* expresses such
an union as that of a sett of jewels placed in the most
exact and regular series. It is applied likewise to the
closest and sincerest friendship. By the same metaphor
the Arabians describe the mutual harmony of society, and the position of an army formed so as to re-
sist the enemy. When disagreement or confusion
arises, they say, *nidámahom, their cord,* or *thread* is
broken.

Ib. *Not approved of: lam jachib.* From hence that
form o imprecation: *chaibatan laho: Let no success
attend him.*

Ib. *Instrument,* &c. The original is, *Penetrating
through the Zend never failed.* Alluding to the
custom of raising fire from an instrument called the

Zend;

Zend; viz. one piece of wood put into the hollow of another, which by rubbing and chafing waxed hot and kindled. This the Arabians efteem an emblem of mutual genius and difpofition. *Zaradufht*, commonly called *Zoroafter*, wrote a book containing the principles and practice of the Perfian religion; to which he gave the title of Zend. This word literally fignifies *a fire-kindler*; intimating that the doctrine therein mentioned, the true divine light, was delivered to him from heaven. In this he was imitated by *Makomet*, who pretended the fame authority, to give the greater fanction to his *Alcoran*. Vid. *Pocock* Not. in *Abul-Faraj. Specim. Hiftor. Arab.* p. 148. and *Prideaux* Connect. P. 1. B. 4. p. 316, &c.

Ib. *Appearance*, &c. Arab. *Nor did any fire of contention rage.* The fame figure taken from the Zend continued.

Ib. *To recite*, &c. Arab. *We mutually draw the extremities of thofe verfes we repeat:* alluding to a number of men affembled together, and to fhew their genius for poetry repeat verfes alternately; like two perfons who draw a rope backwards and forwards, as the original intimates. *Extremities: atráfon.* A word of large conftruction among the Arabians. *Morning and evening* with them are *the extremities* of the *day*. Ennobled in both *extremities*, i. e. *by father and mother*. On the contrary, thofe of the loweft progeny, are called *the extremities of men*. Applied to a traveller; *He contracted his extremities:* i. e. he gathered up his baggage.

Ib. *Entertaining*, &c. The Arabic here is fo expreffive as to fignify, " we were as eager to take our turns as camels are when they go to drink, ftriving which fhall come firft at the water."

Ib. *Enjoy*, &c. The original is the form of a morning falutation, viz. *May your morning compotation be quite agreeable!*

Pag. 43. *Houfhold*, &c. The fcholiaft's interpretation is, " a perfon of noble extraction, munificent to numbers of people, who were always ready to render him the higheft honours."

Ib.

Ib. *Plenteous stream.* His flow of wealth, in the Arab. is compared to rain, which communicates itself to different places and persons of all degrees.

Ib. *Estates and villages.* Arab. Goods not moveable, *viz.* houses, lands, palm-trees.

Ib. *Spring-mansion. How spatious their spring-mansion,* is a proverb among the Arabians, signifying, how do they abound in all the good things of life! how large their habitation! how affluent their riches!

Pag. 44. *Beds : almádgao.* A word applied to *noble-birth : nobiles cubilia,* such as are descended from *mothers of quality.*

Ib. *Strew'd with pebbles : akadda-káddon,* is a pebble of a larger size : *kadídon,* one of a less. Two words applied to multitudes : *viz.* They came and attacked us *kaddon wa-kadídon: great and small, of all ranks and orders, young and old.*

Ib. *Deserted. chálat.* A word applied to death. *viz.* his place *chála, is vacant.* i. e. *He is dead.*

Ib. *Cattle : wealth.* The Arabic literally is, *That which had a voice, and that which was silent, are perished.* i. e. Not only my *live-cattle,* viz. my oxen, my sheep, my camels, are taken from me; but my *mute-substance,* my gold, my silver, my houshold goods are exhausted.

Ib. *Tread the ground.* Arab. Tender-footed, and in pain like a horse whose hoof is worn away by travelling; and instead of proper shoes is shod with pebble stones.

Ib. *Strangle.* The original alludes to that disorder, or inflammation in the throat which stops the breath, and what we call the *quinsie.* This and the foregoing phrase is the same, as the scholiast writes, with *being shod,* not with *real shoes*; and *nourished* with what is not *real nourishment.* In the same sense we read, 1 *Kings* xxii. 27. Feed him [*Michaiah*] with the bread of affliction. Comp. *Isai.* xxx. 20.

Ib. *Alleviating.* Arab. Instead of a plaister to allay the pain of my body, my medicines are such as increase that pain.

Pag.

Pag. 45. *Solacing*, &c. Arab. Inftead of applying any falve or outward means to keep mine eyes from fleeping, I anoint them with watchful and troublefome dreams.

Ib. *Valleys*. Should it be afked why *dwelling in val-leys* was fo bad a fituation? which might rather be efteemed places of greater fafety, more fecured from ftorms and tempefts, and feveral other inconvenien-cies. The Arabian is ready to anfwer, that fuch a fituation is peculiar to thofe of the pooreft and mean-eft rank; where they are concealed from the eye of the world, enjoying themfelves, as well as they are able, in their obfcurity. They choofe fuch dwellings, faith the fcholiaft, *That their fire may not be feen by travellers and ftrangers:* hills and mountains being appropriated to the great and wealthy, who kindle fires there as fignals of hofpitality. Thofe *hofpitable fires*, were named *nirána-l-kóra*. Vid. not. on ℣. 23. of the *Traveller:* an Arabic poem intitled *Tograi*, by L. C.

Ib. *Rough*, &c. The original *kitádon* denotes the *tragacantha, a tree pointed with fharp thorns*; prover-bially applied by the Arabians to the difficulties of life. A figure that is frequently ufed in H. fcripture. *Ifai*. xxxiv. 13. *Thorns* fhall come up in her palaces; in their tabernacles; upon their altars. *Hof.* ix. 6.— x. 8.

Ib. *Kaila*. Vid. not. on *Affemh.* II. p. 32.

Ib. *Poverty*. Arab. *Brother of poverty*. The Ara-bians fay, he is the *brother* of, or to any thing, who is very diligent in profecuting it. He who is engaged in a military life, is the *brother of war*. A jealous perfon, or one who indulges himfelf in trifling fenti-ments, is the *brother of fufpicion*. An effeminate, mean fpirited man, is the *brother of foftnefs and fub-miffion*. The fame phrafe is applied to one in any diftrefs, called the *brother of forrow*. Vid. chap. not. on *Job* v. 7. — and xvii. 14.

Pag. 46. *Entertained*, &c. Arab. Drawing from him his *rhyming joints, or vertebræ*. A thought, peculiar indeed

indeed to an eaftern genius! but not fo extravagant per-
haps, when we confider how great admirers the Arabians
were of poetry; in which they were fo exact, as to
refemble the due compofition of verfes to the joints
of an human body; intimating that the poet's fentiments fhould run eafy, correfponding with each other
in the fame proportion with that which we obferve in
the frame and contexture of our bodies. — The original likewife points out an articulate elegancy of fpeech,
and the proper period with which it fhould terminate:
and that it ought to flow in a rich vein, like water
that iffues in a fteady courfe from a living fpring.

Ib. *Bufinefs*, &c. The poet very elegantly confiders
the great ufe of gold in this particular branch, viz.
The difpatch of bufinefs: intimating that when we have
it not in our power to reward the induftrious, diligence
muft flacken in proportion. The full fenfe of the
Arabic likewife fignifies the brifknefs and alacrity of
our *thoughts*, when after the pains we have taken, the
clear profpect of a recompence is opened to us; a
fight as pleafing to the eye, as that of *a luminous
conjunction of ftars*. The fubftantive of the verb
kárana, *To expedite*, here ufed is applicable to *that
conjunction*. *Free, as thought, chátraton.* The Arabians fay, fuch a thought is *free and vibrating*. They
compare the fhortnefs of life to a vibration. Correfpondent to this is *Pfal.*xc.9. we fpend our years *cemo
begeh, as a tale, tanquam fermo:* rather, as a word that
is fpoken: *As a vapour of the mouth. Chald. Par.*

Pag. 48. *Change the fcene*, &c. The literal verfion
is, *How many full moons hath his* [thy] *face, which refembles the moon, brought low!* By the *full moons*, the
poet facetioufly underftands fuch as are raifed to the
height of glory: and by *the face that refembles the
moon*, the gold that fhines with the fame luftre that
the full moon does. As if he had faid; " So bewitching is the power of gold, that feveral perfons,
in other refpects of worth and efteem, by the influence of money have forfeited that honour by which
they were ufually diftinguifhed.".

Pag,

Pag. 48. Stanz. ix, x. Perfonal actions are here very artfully imputed to *gold:* particularly that fovereign authority by which it governs mankind. *Lord: Máwla.* From this word we fuppofe the African princes have adopted the title of *mouley.* So paffionately defirous are fome men of enriching themfelves, that the poet reprefents them as paying even divine worfhip to *gold. As God — adore thee. Gallat.* Literally, *very great* is thy power. To this verb the Arabians add another of the fame import, viz. *azza,* to fignify the fupreme power of the Deity. *A'zza wa-gallá,* being an ufual form with them, fignifying *that* of the Latins, *Deus optimus maximus.* The words of our Mahometan are a good fatyr againft fuch as put their truft in riches ; plainly fuggefting that they whofe affections are too much placed on earthly treafures, have caft off even *the fear of God.* A crime which holy *Job* with much folemnity protefts, had he been guilty of, *he fhould have denied the God above.* ch. xxxi. 28. And attended with fo very bad circumftances, as to make it very difficult for us [we have our Bleffed Saviour's authority, *Mark* x. 24.] to enter into the kingdom of God.

Pag. 49. *A man,* &c. In thefe and the following words are contained two Arabic fentences ; fuch as are obvious to the meaneft capacity. The firft fhews the principles of an honeft, ingenuous mind, free from low and felfifh motives, and prepared at all times to fulfil engagements. From the other, though delivered in a more figurative way, we learn what will be the event of any thing or action by the figns and tokens that precede it. Correfpondent to what is mentioned the Arabians have two *Adagies,* viz. *Generous actions are derived from generous parents. The wifeft man is he who has a regard to the end. Sent. Arab. Gol. Ed.* p. 54. — 153.

Ib. *Gathered up: fhámmara.* A word common to the Arabians, intimating a readinefs to undertake any expedition : whether to engage in battle, or to fly before the enemy. It is applicable to one who arrogates

gates

gates to himfelf things of great moment, but in the leaft of them is very deficient. Thus *Abul-Chair*, the Egyptian jew, who affumed the character of a fkilful phyfician, when at the fame time he was remarkable for his ignorance, is poetically defcribed, as one who, " *yofhámmiro, gathers up* his garment, with an intent to enter and found the depth of the fea ; but even on the fhore is deftroyed by the boifterous waves." Vid. *Greg. Ab. Phar. Hift. Dyn.* p. 376.

Ib. *Degree of uneafinefs.* Arab. *nófhwato garámin : ebrietas animi nimis cupidi.* Signifying that there arifes as much confufion in the mind of one who ferioufly reflects he has acted an ungenerous part, as if he was really difordered by an intemperate ufe of wine.

Ib. *Curfe : tabban.* Vid. not. *Affemb.* I. p. 15.

Ib. *Hypocrite : al-monáfiko.* From *náfaka : The field-moufe came out of his hole.* Compared to a perfon, who has always fome fubterfuge or other, whenever he is preffed with difficulties. The Arabians call that little animal *jarbówon, quadrator* ; becaufe its cells are difpofed agreeable to the four quarters of the heavens. From hence this proverb, *A crafty man, like the field-moufe is not to be taken at one hole. Plautus*, in his *Truculentus*, writes, *Act.* 4. *Scen.* 4. *⁂*. 15.

Cogitato, mus pufillus quam fit fapiens beftia !
Ætatem qui uni cubili nunquam committit fuam,
Quia fi unum oftium obfideatur, aliud perfugium gerit.

There is another proverb among the Arabians, *viz.* " The mole wandered from *nafaka-ho : it's burrow :*" applied to him whofe thoughts in difputation are fo confufed that he forgets the arguments he intended to urge againft his adverfary. Vid. not. on the *Traveller*, ⁂. 31. L. C. and *Bochart. Hieroz.* L. 3. c. 33. col. 1012. In allufion to the working of moles and conies, *Náficon* fignifies *an hypocrite in religion*, profeffing with his mouth what is not in his heart, being always ready for fome cunning evafion : or, becaufe *outwardly* he is a *believer*, but in reality an *infidel :* like the burrow of a mole, which to appearance is covered, but is deceitfully hollow.

Pag.

Pag. 50. *Bright,* &c. The poet here facetioufly compares the fplendor of gold, to that pleafing countenance in the female objeƈt when addreffes are made
to her: and at the fame time that palenefs mixed with
yellow which the lover's face frequently difcovers.

Ib. *Of truth tenacious.* Arab. *Poffeffors of truth.* A
form with the orientals, fignifying fuch as are *endow-*
ed with judgement and knowledge, viewing the things of
this world with the eye of truth: which, they fay, *is*
incumbent on every man to defend.

Ib. *Call for indignation.* The Arabic here has a peculiar emphafis: as if the mifer's thoughts inftigated,
and in a manner compelled him to defy the power of
God: fuggefting to him that his fubftance *irtákaba,*
mounts, or *raifes* him above the Almighty's difplea-
fure. *To mount or climb up to a crime.* Arab. is *To at-*
tempt or commit it with an high hand. To climb up
to covetoufnefs, to be influenced by it. To fpeak as an
Orator, to mount up to the art of fpeaking. To mount the
wings of an Oftrich, to be expeditious in our aƈtions.

Ib. *Amputation.* i. e. Cutting of the hand for theft.
This was an injunƈtion of *Mahomet's, Alcor.* ch. v.
ỳ. 44. viz. *If a man or woman be guilty of theft, cut off*
the hands of both: which he calls, *an exemplary punifh-*
ment from God. From hence this imprecation againft
an adverfary; *May God cut off thine hand.*

Ib. *Break,* &c. *The date,* when ripe, the Arabians fay,
pofek, breaks through the cortex. Applied to one who is
prepared to engage in any wickednefs. This reprefentation of the date, in *Schulten's* opinion, gives much
force and eloquence to thofe texts in *Prov.* xiii. 3. and
Ezek. xvi. 25. where the Hebrew radix *pafak* is ufed.
He that keepeth his mouth, keepeth his life: *but*
pofek, he that *openeth wide* his lips, fhall have de-
ftruƈtion. Thou haft made thy beauty to be abhor-
red, and *tepaffeki, haft opened* thy feet to every one
that paffed by. i. e. *Erupifti* extra *corticem* omnis vir-
tutis: *thou haft violently broken through the guards that*
are placed for the fecurity of virtue and honour.

Ib. *Shrink,* &c. The Arabic here expreffes fuch a
terror

terror as not only difturbs the mind, but contracts
even the features of the face: the fame word that *Ma-
bomet* threatens thofe with who do not believe in a life
to come. "At the mention of God, he faith, their
hearts, *ifhmaázzat*, are contracted." *Alcor.* ch. xxxix. 45.

Pag. 51. *Envy,* Arab. *Ráfhikon :* One who is fkilful
in darting : applied to thofe who caft an evil eye,
as it were a dart, on other men's profperity.

Ib. *Common form. Maádha-lláhi : Refugium Dei!*
The refuge of God I flee to: or; *God forbid!* an expreffion frequently in the mouth of an Arabian, (as
well as other nations) to avert any divine judgement.
The two laft chapters of the *Alcoran* are by the Commentators entitled, *Confugiaria,* or, *Capita Averrun-
cantia ;* becaufe they both begin with the form *aówdho
bi-lláhi, confugio ad Deum :* where *Mahomet* inftructs
his followers to fuplicate God's protection againft certain calamities which he there fpecifies.

Ib. *How ftrangely formed,* &c. The poet from
fpeaking of the happinefs that would attend us, did
not our love of money rife to excefs, in this ftanza
fets forth the bad ufe that is too often made of it
when not properly applied. Intimating that the fordid mifer's treafures are of no moment, even in the
moft difficult circumftances, till fuch time as they
can break from their confinement, and make their
efcape like a fugitive, who by fome lucky accident
has gained his liberty.

Ib. *Higheft mountain. To throw down any one from
a rock or mountain,* is proverbially the fame as wifh-
ing the greateft evil imaginable may happen to him.
This is the poet's wifh here, that fuch may be the
fate of gold, or rather, of him who paffionately
admires it.

Pag. 52. *The condition,* &c. A proverb, to incite a
perfon to perform his promife without fubterfuge or
evafion.

Ib. *Prefented,* &c. Arab. *I breathed upon him with,* &c.
An expreffion, though ufed here in a good fenfe, yet
generally in a bad one. Thus *Mahomet* threatens
the

the difobedient with the *breath of divine punifhment*. No doubt but he does this in imitation of the holy fcripture, where the fame phrafe is frequently mentioned. Comp. 2 *Sam.* xxii. 16. and *Pfal.* xviii. 15. *The blaft of the breath of his noftrils.*

Ib. *Guardian*, &c. The verfes referred to are thofe which are called *Averruncate*, in which are contained the form of averting any impendent calamity or judgement. Vid. not. on *Common form*, p. 63.

Ib. *Morning-adventure: mágdan.* This word is proverbially applied to a fon who in all refpects imitates his father: thus expreffed, "He forfakes not his father either, *magdan*, in his *morning-adventure*; or *maráhan*, *his evening-retirement*.

Pag. 53. *May thy life*, &c. From the verb *Hayya, vixit*, one of the moft refpectful compliments is intended by the Arabians, as well as other nations, *viz. Hayyáca-allàho: God preferve thy life.*

Pag. 54. *Gate*, &c. Arab. *To knock at the gate of comfort.* The gate is frequently applied as an entrance to find out what is really fact and truth. *Hai Ebn Yokdhan* blames thofe who would feek for truth in the common and vulgar way, and not be at the pains of *entering min bábihi: into it's gate.* p. 193. *Ebn Sina*, or *Avicenan*, tells us, that by experience he had learned the ways of curing difeafes, not to be numbered; which he expreffes by opening *abwábahom, their gates.* Ab. *Pharag. Hift. Dynaft.* p. 350.

Ib. *Like Camel*, &c. Arab. *I throw my rein over my back:* a proverb, fignifying his liberty to go whither and when he pleafed. Like the Arabians, who to keep their camels from wandering, faften the extreme part of their head-ftall to the knee; but loofen and throw it over their backs when they fend them into large and free pafture.

Ib. *Inftructed*, &c. *Abuzeid* being defirous of excufing his pretended lamenefs, as if he was not guilty of hypocrify, intimates that this artifice was not of his own inventing, but that *nature* fuggefted it to him.

4

ASSEMBLY IV.

ENTITLED

DAMIATENSIS.

HARITH the fon of *Hemmam* in the narrative he gives of himfelf is this. The courfe of my travels brought me as far as *Dimját*, in that year which was remarkable for *confufion and tumult*. But the circumftances which I was then favoured with were fo eafy, fo full and profperous, that the poor man was pleafed and rejoiced whenever I caft my eye on him, though it was in the flighteft manner; and I was much efteemed and beloved by numerous friends and acquaintance. The garments I was adorned with, were rich and fplendid; formed in fo juft and elegant a manner, as readily to diftinguifh they were wrought by the moft experienced and curious artift. They appeared to the eye as if bubbles of water were continually flowing over them. And fo delicate and happy was every paffage of my life, that my countenance and all the features belonging to it fhewed themfelves with the fame alacrity, and to the fame advantage with thofe of the bride; when, the veil being taken from her, fhe is brought to her bed-chamber, expecting the tender embraces of her beloved bridegroom. The companions I made choice of in my travels, were thofe in whom I could place the greateft truft and confidence; men of the moft fociable and benevolent difpofitions. Did any difputes or quarrels arife, they were always ready to interpofe, and fuccefsful in *compofing* them. So unanimous in their opinions, that they adhered as clofe to them as children

E   *fucking*

sucking at their mothers breasts. So remarkably even and steddy in their behaviour, that one might resemble them to the *teeth of a comb*, placed in the most exact and distinct order. Their wills and affections being so mutually joined together, and conspiring always in the same sentiments, that you would be ready to think, the same soul possessed each man's separate body. This happy state enabled us, wherever we travelled, to direct our course in the swiftest and most easy manner: for the camels we made use of were such as moved with the utmost readiness and expedition. When we entered the house of any one, that we might take some rest and refreshment; so far from giving uneasiness to the family by continuing longer than our necessity required; without the least delay we *made all the haste* that was possible to remove, and to forward our journey. So determined in our motions, that our progress was quick, not only in the day, but even in the *dark night*, when we did not suffer our camels to slacken or retard their paces. So dark, that you might compare it to the colour of a *black crow*. Thus did we continue our journey *till the day began to break*, and the morning to spread it's *rosy colour*. We were now sensible of a very great fatigue, which our night-travel had occasioned : and our inclination to rest and sleep being strong and increasing, we had the good fortune to come at a tract of land exceedingly pleasant and delicate ; adorned with little hills, covered with an agreeable verdure, to be compared with a fine rich meadow, or a well disposed garden ; refreshed with cool, languishing breezes of wind, such as blow from the east in the time of equinox. This place we judged to be most convenient for our purpose, and therefore made choice of it, not only that our camels, [for which we had a peculiar regard, as they were of a beauteous kind] might find rest and ease ; but we ourselves too might possess an agreeable station for such repose as would enable us the better to prosecute our journey. No sooner had our promiscuous company descended to this resting-place, and the groans

of

of wearied camels, and the fnoring of my fellow-travellers were filenced; but I heard a clear diftinct voice utter itfelf to one of them, in thefe words, "I fhould be glad to know what is thy manner and conduct of life with regard to the men of this age in general, and particularly thofe who are thy neighbours and acquaintance?" To which he made this anfwer.

"As a fhepherd keeps a watchful eye over his flock, for fear any of them fhould wander and go aftray; fo is it my ufual cuftom carefully to obferve the man who makes any addrefs to me, that I may be refpectful to him, even though he fhould deviate from the ftrict rules of juftice. And if he be of a morofe, fierce temper, I then *treat him* with feveral marks of friendfhip. If my companion be of a quarrelfom difpofition, fo as to difturb the harmony of fociety; I have that command of my felf to bear with his infirmity; and I cannot but fhew my love to a perfon, for whom I have a real affection, even though he be the *occafion* to me *of* much grief and uneafinefs. A friend that is tender and compaffionate, I prefer to a brother or near relation. To an acquaintance I am punctual and exact in rendering what is his juft due, though he does not return me the tenth part of what I have a right to demand. To a ftranger who begs for relief, I make large prefents; and he who is in a low, *inferior* ftation, is entitled to my particular affiftance. If I have a night-affociate whofe converfation with me is free and eafy, I pay him as much reverence as I would do to a *governor* or dictator. If one who recommends himfelf to me by his humanity, and the proficiency he hath made in good learning, and a proper education; I fhew him the fame refpect as if he was my prince or general. Thofe perfons who have any knowledge of me, find me at all times willing to do them fuch acts of kindnefs as are confiftent with what is good and equitable. And fhould I meet with a conftant attendant who makes no difficulty of fojourning with me in my feveral ftages, I am prepared to affift him in every neceffitous cafe to the utmoft of my

fubsubftance. Do I happen to converfe with one whofe averfion to me is fuch that to injure me, he would purfue the moft *violent meafures:* my bufinefs then is to foften my fpeech, and difcourfe with him in the mildeft terms. But if I am fecure of a perfon, fo as to be fatisfied that his abilities are not of any moment; it is my cuftom to addrefs myfelf frequently to him, and in much civility enquire of his health and welfare. Does my behaviour at any time merit a reward? inftead of being gratified with what I might reafonably expect, I make myfelf eafy with the *fmalleft tender* of kindnefs: for as it is given by way of recompence, I make no difficulty of receiving it. If I am fo unfortunate, that inftead of fair and equitable treatment, I meet with hard and unjuft meafures; and inftead of tendernefs and affection, I am heavily loaded with oppreffion; it is my way not to complain, nor does my refentment rife fo high as to meditate revenge: no, *though I am provoked by a man of the moft virulent difpofition."*

The anfwer his companion made was this: "O my fon, what canft thou expect but mifery and unhappinefs from fuch principles as thou haft advanced? on the contrary, it is my ftedfaft opinion, that fo far from expofing one's reputation to public cenfure, we fhould tenacioufly adhere to what is laudable and of true efteem; and the utmoft of our ambition fhould be, to afpire after fuch concerns as are *noble and generous.* For inftance, if my circumftances are full and plenteous, I am not profufe to thofe, who have it not in their power to return the favour. Should I meet with an infolent, proud man; I could not efteem him worthy of any mark of my diftinction or refpect. Do I appeal to a perfon for juftice, and he refufes to vindicate me from the injury I fuffer; my refentment is fuch, that I cannot exprefs the leaft fincere affection for him? He who difregards thofe duties which are incumbent on brothers or near relations to perform; muft not prefume I fhould pay that regard to him, as I would do to one who hath a juft title to
bro-

brotherly kindneſs. Does any one imagine I ſhall be forward to aſſiſt him in diſtreſs, when he is ſenſible how much he hath deceived me, and fruſtrated thoſe hopes I had conceived of him? He who is guilty of a *breach of acquaintance and friendſhip*, is not to ſuppoſe I can have a true regard for him. Neither do I diſtinguiſh a man by mild and gentle treatment, who is ſo fooliſh as not to pay that reſpect which he owes, and which is due to me. If I have *recourſe to* a perſon for his patronage and protection, placing my truſt and confidence in him; and inſtead of relieving, he betrays me; I have no longer any communication with him. If I muſt converſe with thoſe who are mine enemies, I am not ſo prodigal of my friendſhip as to admit them to any part of it. Nor am I ſo inſenſible of the ungenerous treatment of an adverſary, as not to threaten him if he perſiſts in it. Should any one rejoice at my misfortunes, my temper is not ſo *ſmooth* and indolent, as to paſs it by without a proper reſentment. And if I knew the man who would be pleaſed and inſult over me at my death, I muſt look upon him with as much diſdain, as on a perſon that was perverſe and diſtorted both in body and mind. Should it be enquired whether I am deſirous of receiving preſents and gratuities; my anſwer would be, From thoſe only who have an affectionate love for me. Was I reduced by poverty to a ſtate of diſtreſs, I ſhould not ſeek my remedy but from ſuch perſons, whoſe tenderneſs and compaſſion I might ſecurely truſt to. Neither would I cultivate an intimate friendſhip with one, who was not ready to *ſuccour me* in my indigent circumſtances. Did I know a man who was deſirous of, and ardently wiſhed for my death, Can you imagine he had any title to my hearty and ſincere intentions? He who is ſo uncharitable as not to refreſh my empty *pockets* with a neceſſary ſupply, muſt not expect I ſhould *compliment* him with my beſt wiſhes for his happineſs and proſperity. Nor am I *laviſh* in my commendations to him, who in any reſpect hath injured my character.

Is

Is there any man, let me afk, who, if his judgement was required, would be fo partial as to determine, that I ought to be liberal and beneficent; and that thou hadft the liberty of treafuring up, and increafing thy ftore? That it was my duty to be of a mild, gentle difpofition; and that thou mighteft indulge a rough, intractable temper? That I fhould be of fo tender a nature, as to melt and diffolve at the thoughts of every calamity; and that no object of diftrefs fhould foften thy congealed bowels? That my love and affection for private, or public profperity fhould be flagrant, kindled with a pure flame; and that thine fhould be cool and languid, without the leaft zeal for what is truly advantageous? That this is an unjuft and unreafonable way of acting, I call God himfelf to witnefs. The words that we fpeak, fhould be weighed and balanced in a true, juft fcale: and the *actions* we engage in, confidered with the fame care and exactnefs. Such are the expedients neceffary to fecure us from treachery and *fraud*; and to prevent any hatred or ill defign againft us. Do not I fpeak that which is juft and proper? For, what reafon is there to be affigned, why I fhould gratify thee with feveral favours, and fupply thee with one draught after another, till thy thirft is quite fatiated; if thou art of fo ingrateful a temper a s to load me with repeated afflictions? Shall I be ready to eafe thee of thy heavy burden, when thou fheweft no regard to me labouring under the fame preffure? Shall I make it my ftudy to add to thy ftore, and increafe thy acquifitions, when thy time is employed to wound and injure me in my property? In thy neceffity fhall my bounty be freely poured out, like water flowing with an uninterrupted courfe; and in my diftreffed circumftances wilt thou be fo little affected as to bid me, without any affiftance, go and provide for my felf? Were thefe principles to be admitted, what rules fhould we have to compare juftice with injuftice, righteous dealing with oppreffion? By the fame way of reafoning we may maintain, that our countenance
                                                        fhould

should appear placid and serene to him who looks on us with a dark, cloudy aspect; which would be as great an absurdity as to affirm, that the sun should shine bright when it is overcast with a thick cloud. Or, that our love and affection should exert themselves to the highest degree, in favour of those, whose hatred and malice are directed against us with the utmost violence. For where will you find one animated with such a noble, *generous warmth*, as to be perfectly easy and undisturbed, when he meets with *base*, undeserving *treatment?* Excellent and divine were those words of *thy father*, when he said:

I.

Does any one with gen'rous soul possess'd,
Distinguish me with truest signs of love?
Should not my gratitude exert it's pow'r,
The bounteous mark of friendship to repay?

II.

Is my associate liberal and free?
He's sure to find me equally dispos'd,
But if the tender of his bounty's small;
He must expect the same deficient hand.

III.

Free from the dark and fraudulent designs
Of artful men my conduct I preserve.
He is the worst, the vilest of mankind,
Who studies *to* detract *from righteous truth.*

IV.

The tyrant *who delights t' oppress and spoil;*
JUSTICE, *when he's oppress'd, forbids complaint.*
The wretch, whose words are scandal, must not grieve,
When injur'd by the voice of public FAME.

V.

I take no pleasure in those treach'rous arts;
Those schemes of policy to deceive mankind.
Th' applause which crafty circumventors *gain,*
Tho' grateful to their ears, is my disdain.

E 4

As

VI.

As common duties are of mutual force ;
The rules of equity I muſt tranſgreſs:
To his injunctions ſhould I homage pay,
From which he claims a freedom abſolute ?

VII.

He who is vers'd in baſe, perfidious arts,
And loud pretences to affliction makes ;
Vainly imagines I'm his cred'lous ſlave,
T' embrace for truth all his fictitious love.

VIII.

So ſtrange and inconſiſtent are his thoughts,
He does not, will not, rightly apprehend,
That I ſhall readily diſcharge the debt,
By the ſame meaſure, and in kind the ſame.

IX.

Is he ſo negligent as not to pay
The common duties which thy ſtation claims ?
With deteſtation from his preſence flee,
As from a nauſeous corpſe dug from his grave.

X.

In friendſhip if he's outwardly ſincere,
With all the marks of honour and reſpect ;
And yet ſo ſubtle, he betrays his friend :
Familiar converſe cautiouſly avoid.

XI.

Does thy companion find thy indigence
Is ſuch, as labours for his full ſupply ?
Your mutual bonds of love, tho' ne'er ſo ſtrong,
Will ſoon be chang'd, and loſe their former ſtrength.

Harith ibn Hemmam ſaid, when with the moſt diligent attention I had heard, and to the beſt of my remembrance collected the particulars of their mutual diſcourſe, I was extremely deſirous to have a thorough knowledge *of their perſons.* No ſooner did *the morning*

ing shew itself bright and clear after the rising of the sun, and *the light spread* itself through the air; but I rose from my bed before the loaded travellers with their caravans, or even the *early crows* had made their appearance. I then directed my course towards a certain night-voice which reached my ears; and at last I came to a clear, distinct view of two faces. By a flight cast of the eye I perceived that it was *Abuzeid* and his son engaged in close conversation with each other: both of them clothed in old ragged garments. And knowing very well that the son as well as the father might be trusted with any secret, I resolved to associate with them in my night's-discourse, in such an agreeable, humorous way, as to make it a pleasing and delightful entertainment. Therefore without farther ceremony, I addressed them with the same eagerness that a person would attempt a thing for which he has a real and true affection; being very sensible of their courteous and mild disposition, especially should I condole with them on the necessitous condition they then laboured under: For this reason I indulged them the full liberty of *making themselves my companions*: and of applying to their use, as they judged convenient, whatever was my property though of ever so *great or small concern*. After this indulgence, I applied myself to the company of travellers, and informed them of the real value and excellence of those two men, with a design *to promote* their liberality; *to enrich* them by their beneficence: and treat them with the same kind reception, as they would do their intimate friends and companions. We happened to be in a place, to which travellers in the night resort for their refreshment, that they may be more able to prosecute their journey the next day. From hence we could observe distinctly the buildings of several villages, and have a clear view of the *hospitable fires*. As soon as *Abuzeid* saw a full purse, and poverty with it's miserable circumstances shaken and dissipated; he said to me, I must ingenuously confess to you that my body is grown squalid and dirty; and the smell arising

ing from it naufeous and loathfom : permit me then
to go and bathe in fome neighbouring village, where
I may have time fufficient to cleanfe and purify myfelf, a matter of importance to me, and requires no
fmall confideration. When I told him, he was at his
own liberty ; and under no obligation as to any particular time ; only to return, after having difpatched
his bufinefs, fo foon as his conveniency would permit him ; the anfwer he made, was, Affure yourfelf
my return to you fhall be expeditious ; and allow me
the comparifon, fwifter than the twinkling of an eye.
He then began to run with the fame fwiftnefs, as one
of thofe generous horfes does that is trained up for *the
courfe*. And for fear his fon fhould delay and lofe
time, he repeated his call to him, Make hafte, make
hafte. But not having the leaft fufpicion of his de-
ceiving, and his intention to efcape from us, our de-
lays were frequent, making obfervations on him with
as much attention, as thofe feafts that depend on the
appearance of the moon are obferved by the *watchers*;
and with the fame diligence that thofe forragers ufe,
when they are difpatched to feek and provide neceffary fupplies and refrefhment for an army. Thus were
we employed even till *the day* began to decline, and
the light to difappear. But when we had waited with
full and longing expectation, and the *fun* almoft *darkened* ; I faid to my companions, furely we make too
much delay, and have protracted our courfe, fo as
to lofe a great deal of time. I am fatisfied the man's
whole contrivance has been to treat us in a fraudulent
manner. Therefore be as expeditious as poffible to
prepare for our journey, without any concerh or regard for one whofe *outward behaviour* was plaufible
and honeft ; but the event fhews, he is a perfon of
a bafe, difingenuous temper. Being then as eager to
move as a bird with wings expanded is, to fly, I
rofe up in hafte to load my camel. And whilft I was
collecting together what materials were neceffary for
travelling, I found that *Abuzeid* had wrote this infcription on my camel's faddle :

My

My greateſt ; beſt ſupport ! no parallel
Can equal thee among the ſons of men.
Eſteem me not a wand'ring fugitive,
Prompted by raſh diſdain, or wantonneſs.
For from my birth, like camels richly fed,
My keeper left, I've various ways purſued.

This infcription, he faid, I gave to the company,
to read ; and that it might be fome plea for my ac-
cufing him of fo much ungenerous behaviour. And
being in high admiration of the *fabulous* and pleafing
account he had given of himfelf, they petitioned in
the ftrongeft terms, that *that* might *make an atonement* for his crime. We then proceeded on our journey, not knowing what affociates he might have fub-
ftituted to deal with us, in the fame ludicrous manner.

NOTES

N O T E S

O N

A S S E M B L Y IV.

ENTITLED

D A M I A T E N S I S.

P AG. 65. *Dimjat,* or *Damjata,* once a famous city in Egypt : the fame that *Stephens* calls Ταμίαϑις· *Gol.* ad *Alfrag.* p. 148. *Jerem.* ii. 16. we read of that city by the name of *Tahpanhes*: lxx. Τάφυας. which . gave title to a queen of Egypt, 1 *King.* xi. 19. fuppofed to be the *Daphne Pelufiace:* where St. *Jerom* writes, from an ancient tradition, the prophet *Jeremiah* was ftoned by the Jews. Vid. *Schultens. Ind. Geogr.* in *Vitam Saladini.*

Ib. *Confufion and tumult.* The Arab. words (as ufual with our Author through all his *Affemblies*) correfpond in found, viz. *Hiyát wa-Miyát :* From hence the Arabians, when they would exprefs the utmoft diftrefs that men can be involved in, fay, *tebáyatow wa-temáyatow : inter fe ultro citroque impulerunt, et repulerunt : nothing but the utmoft diforder and confufion amongft them.*

Ib. *Compofing,* &c. The original is one of the Arabian *Adagies* ; viz. *They broke the ftaff of diffenfion. The ftaff, Abu Obeid* writes, is proverbially applied to *fociety*; and the *breaking* of it, to *diffenfion.* In this fenfe he obferves, when a perfon *breaks the ftaff of the Mofelmen,* it is the fame, as, *he deferts their communion and fellowfhip.* In holy Scripture *a ftaff* is mention'd as an emblem of power and authority,

which

which is abufed in the hand of a tyrant and an op-
preffor as, *Ifai.* ix. 4. *Thou haft broken the ftaff of his
fhoulder,* i. e. thou haft fubdued the tyrant's infolence.
and ch. xiv. 5. *The Lord hath broken the ftaff of the
wicked. How is the ftrong ftaff broken!* *Jer.* xlviii. 17.

Pag. 66. *Sucking,* &c. The Arabic is very ftrong and
figurative, together with the *Paranomofia,* in which
the Arabians much delight, viz. *fucking, afáwika-'l-
wifáki, the milky draughts of harmony.* With them are
thefe frequent metaphors, *To fuck the breafts of learning, of virtue,* &c. and *of vice, injuftice,* &c. In
the fame Eaftern phrafe we read *Ifai.* lxi. 16. *Thou
fhalt fuck the milk of the Gentiles, and the breaft of
kings.* And lxvi. 11. *That ye may fuck the breafts of
her confolations.* This will fuggeft to every member
of the Univerfity of Cambridge, who makes, as he
ought to do, a juft and regular proficiency in acade-
mic ftudies, what nourifhment he hath, or ought to
receive from the breafts of *Alma Mater.*

Ib. *Teeth of a comb.* This comparifon intimates
an equality of mind to do good in whatever ftation
we are placed : on the contrary, *Like the teeth of an
afs,* when the mind is fixed and intent on doing evil.

Ib. *Made all the hafte,* &c. The phrafe here is, *We
fnatched, or ftole delay.* When an heifer lows in a
mild, gentle manner, the Arabs fay, *She fteals her
lowing.* When a difcourfe is drawn up flightly and
carelefsly, they pronounce it, *A ftolen difcourfe.*

Ib. *Dark night,* Arab. *When the night was in its
youth,* i. e. in the beginning of the night, when for
want of the moon the clouds are very dark : the allufion is made to thofe who are young, their hair being
then blacker than when they advance in years. Or, as
the commentator *Tebleb* writes, The Author may refer to the firft night of the month, which is in it's
youth, and dark in the beginning of it's age. The
Arabic *Shabáb, youth,* from *Shábba, arfit, flagravit,*
beautifully expreffes that ardour, that natural heat and
brifknefs which accompany our younger days.

Ib.

.. Ib. *Black crow.* Arab. *In it's skin resembling a crow.* The comparison is poetically applied to one who hath long black hair : and to a woman wearing her spreading veil. *Godáfon,* the word here used, in the 1st conj. *gadafa,* is, *To be liberal,* or *profuse.* And in the 4th, *To let the veil hang loose.* The Arabians indulge their genius so much as to express *a very dark night,* by *the wing of darkness hanging loose. The skin of the night,* they say, is *it's darkness :* on the contrary, *The skin of the day, it's bright countenance. The vast extended firmament,* they call, *The skin of the air.* The Poet *Asedeus,* lamenting the punishment that was inflicted on him, viz. *The shaving of his head,* writes,

> *The crow that grac'd the beauty of my head,*
> *I'm now depriv'd of, and expos'd to scorn.*
> *Their pleasure was the same as gathering grapes,*
> *In clusters heavy, pendulous and ripe.*

The same thought is pursued by another Poet, in this devout strain :

> *To God I make this strong request,*
> *Not to deprive me of my crow :*

i. e. That I may not die in the vigor of my youth.

Ib. *Day-break.* Arab. *Till the night put off her youthful dress :* i. e. her black robes. *Rosy colour.* Arab. *it's red tincture.* In allusion, as *Schultens* supposes, to those Arabian ladies who stain with that colour their nails, and extreme parts of their fingers. From hence, *Tinctured in the extremities of her fingers,* is the same as if you said, *a female Arabian.* And so careful are the Arabs to have their wives distinguished, that it is a maxim with them, *Do not marry a woman that neglects to stain her fingers and eyes.*

Pag. 67. *Treat him,* &c. The Arabic is finely expressed, viz. *Abdholo : I am prodigal of my friendship.* The same verb is applied to *eagerness* and *excess,* viz. *I am prodigal of,* or, *I lay out, all my study.*

7. *I am*

I am prodigal, or, *I make a sacrifice of my very soul.*
I am, saith an Arabian, speaking like a brave warrior,
prodigal of my countenance in battle: i. e. I expose myself to the utmost danger; *but careful to preserve it
when I am in no engagement.*

Ib. *Occasion of,* &c. Arab. Proverbially, *Though
he give me hot water to drink.*

Ib. *Inferior,* &c. Arab. *To the second rider,* [i. e.
one who rides behind me on the same beast] *I give the
best entertainment.*

Ib. *Governor.* Arab. *Amír,* or, *Emír,* a title of
honour which the Arabians use when they profess to
oblige any man with their best offices. · *Thou art my
Emír:* i. e. My ruler and director.

Pag. 68. *Violent Measures:* Arab. *Bake me in a
frying-pan.*

Ib. *Smallest tender,* &c. *Lafáon: Any thing, though
never so inconsiderable, a little dust,* or *fileing of gold.*
From hence the proverb, *Al lafáo gaira-'l-wafái:
Pulvisculus, non complementum. Only dust: no satisfaction: when a person is amused with words, and cannot have common justice.*

Ib. *Though provoked,* &c. Arab. *Though I am bit
by a serpent of the fiercest and most dangerous species.*
Such are those with variegated spots of black and
white.

Ib. *Noble and generous: Danínon: Whatever is ob-
tained and preserved (avarè,) with the greatest care.*
Such things the Arabians call *Danáyino:* by which
word they distinguish *the peculiar properties of God:*
according to their tradition, *To him belong (Dánáon)
creatures highly esteemed: (quas avarè, habet,) These he
suffers to live and die in safety:* i. e. They are his peculiar beloved, his principal objects for which he is
solicitous.

Pag. 69. *Breach,* &c. Arab. *He who breaks my chains,*
or *bonds.*

Ib. *Recourse to,* &c. Arab. *I do not obsequiously
yield my reins,* or *head-stall to him who betrays (dhimámi)
my trust.* Both Jews and Christians when subject to
the

·the Mahometans were diftinguifhed by the name of *Ablo Dhímmatin, Populi Clintelæ, vel Tributarij. Ab. Farag.* p. 336.

Ib. *Smooth: afmacao: enodis fum:* i. e. I am not like a piece of wood that is fo exactly formed as not to have the leaft *knot,* or excrefcence.

Ib. *Succour me:* Arab. Who would not *yafoddo, ftop my gap:* a phrafe of the fame meaning is, *Sadda, be ftopped,* or prevented *the breaking* of his back-bone: i. e. He affifted him in his extreme neceffity. He ftopped the gaping of his hunger: or, he fupplied him with provifions.

Ib. *Pocket: widon: veffel, cafe,* or *box.* To ftuff or fill a man's *veffel,* is the fame as, *To make him large prefents.*

Ib. *Compliment,* &c. *Doáon: precatio,* from which, *Dáin: qui faufta precatur: health and happinefs* to any one, is the word the Mahometans fubfcribe to their epiftles, efpecially when they write to men of note and family.

Ib. *Lavifh,* &c. Arab. By way of contraft to the foregoing fentence; *Nor do I pour out a bottle of water on him, who had emptied and wafted mine.* There is an Arab. Adagy, viz. *His veffel leffened:* i. e. He loft part of his property.

Pag. 70. *Actions:* Arab. *We fhould cut the fhoe according to its model:* which is fpoken as a proverb. There is another of the fame force, viz. *Our feet are in their fhoes:* i. e. We are like to them in every thing.

Ib. *Fraud: Tegábonon:* This is the title of the fixty-fourth chap. of the *Alcoran,* viz. *Mutual deceit.* For at the day of judgement, the Mahometans fay, the *faithful* fhall deceive the *unbelievers,* by taking their place in Paradife, which by bad conduct in life they had forfeited.

71. *Generous warmth: búrron: ingenuus. Treatment: Chóttaton: a line, rule,* or *condition,* to direct us. *Gjeubarri Lexic.* to give us the force of the words: *búrron,* and *chóttaton:* quotes this fentence

of

of *Taábela Sjerran*, viz. When there are [*chottatáni*] *two conditions*, either captivity and reproach, or blood: furely death to [*búrron*] *a man of an ingenuous fpirit* is more agreeable.

Ib. *Bafe treatment:* Arab. Condition of *chásfon:* *injury:* fuch as arifes from the want of provifion; when any beaft, for inftance, is kept a whole night without refrefhment: which gave occafion to a Poet's comparing an *afs* with a *ftake* faftened to the ground, as if they were both vile in nature, and no regard to be had to one more than the other: and, as if they were equally ftupid, fo as not to be fenfible of any *injury* that could be done to them:

Two of the vileft objects when opprefs'd,
With refignation all th' oppreffion bear;
A village-wand'ring *afs*, and faplefs *ftake.*
The *afs*, if faften'd to his ftubborn cord,
Tho' pinch'd with [*chasfon*] *hunger*, yet makes no
    complaint.
In the fame ftupid, fenfelefs ftate remains
The *ftake*; tho' bruis'd with th' hammer's frequent
    ftrokes,
Contufion fuffers, no reluctance fhews.

Ib. *Thy father: Abuzeid* intimates himfelf.

Ib. *Should not,* &c. Arab. *Should not I build upon his foundation?* A proverb with the Arabians for making mutual returns in the fame kind; whether it be *fincerity to him who is fincere:* or, *deceitfulnefs to him who deceives* us.

Ib. *Equally difpofed:* The literal Arabic is, *I mete out to my friend, according to his meafure to me, let it be large or deficient.* This, as *Schultens* writes, correfponds with our Saviour's words, vii *Mat.* 2. *With what meafure ye mete, it fhall be meafured to you again.* But there is this difference: our Saviour applies the words to rafh judgement and hypocrify; the Arabian [if according to the fenfe of the proverb mentioned above] to retaliating *evil for evil,* as well as *good for good.*

Ib.

Ib. *Detract*: *lá 'ochássiro*: *non detraho*: fill up the measure, [i. e. Give every one his due] that ye may not be numbered *min-al-mocksirína*, among the *detractors*: is a precept in the *Alcoran*, *Sur*. xxvi. 180.

Ib. *Studies*, &c. The Arab. here is expressed in a proverbial form, though not very clear to the reader, viz. *Whose day suffers damage more than it's mother*, viz. *Whose second day does more injustice than yesterday*, which is called the parent of the following one: i. e. Who every day grows more and more injurious.

Ib. *The tyrant*, &c. The Arabic is, *Every one who expects fruit from me, gathers only that which he hath planted*. Fruit: *gánan*: from *gána*, To gather fruit. But this verb points out another sense, viz. *To be false, to calumniate*: and *gánin* denotes an unjust man, or a tyrant. It is a proverb with the Arabians, *igtáni má garásta*: *Gather what thou hast planted*: or, *Reap what thou hast sown*.

Ib. *Circumventors*: The Arabic alludes to a proverb, viz. *Complosio circumventi*: When one party, though he is deceived in the bargain, *strikes hands with the other to confirm the agreement*. To such deceitful methods our Author applies *conversation* and *fraudulent commerce* of all kinds.

Pag. 72. *Pretences*, &c. i. e. The dissembler who [*Arab*.] *mixes his love*: alluding to wine diluted with water.

Ib. *Credulous*, &c. Arab. *He imagines I cannot discern his false clothing*: i. e. His dissimulation.

Ib. *Familiar converse*, &c. Arab. *Put on him the garment of one who abhors his familiarity*. The same phrase is used in other respects, viz. *He put on the garment of one going away*: i. e. He went away. *He put on the garment of despair*: i. e. He was in the utmost despair. *The garment of famine, is, extreme famine*. To clothe *with salvation, with shame, with blackness, with trembling*, &c. we know are expressions frequent in the H. Scripture.

Ib. *Of their persons*: Arab. *Of their eye, with, or before the eye*, and *beyond the eye*, are phrases denoting a man's *presence*, or *absence*.

Ib.

Ib. *The morning:* Arab. *The fon of* [*dhocbái*] *the fcorching* SUN : a word that *Ibn Doreid* applies to the uneafinefs of a guilty confcience, viz. " He who cafts off fhame, or defpifes what is facred, treafures up to his foul a repentance more uneafy than the heat *al-dhócai, of the fcorching fun.*"

Pag. 73. *Light fpread,* &c. Arab. *When the light had clothed the air.* Vid. Not. above.

Ib. *Early crows: The morning vigilance of the crow,* is ufed as a proverb. The expreffion in the original is fomewhat peculiar, viz. I rofe *not as the morning crow :* i. e. *I rofe before him. Couragious, not as Alexander :* i. e. *More couragious.*

Ib. *Making,* &c. Arab. *Of placing themfelves on my feat.*

Ib. *Great or fmall.* The Arab. words *cothron* and *collon : plenty* and *fcarcenefs,* by way of adagy diftinguifh things *good* or *bad,* of the *bigbeft* or *loweft value.*

Ib. *To promote,* &c. Arab. *That they might fhake their fruitful trees over them. A tree loaden with fruit,* being a favourite emblem of *a rich man,* among the Arabians.

Ib. *Enrich them,* &c. Arab. *Overpower,* or *immerfe them in their beneficence.*

Ib. *Hofpitable fires.* A defcription of which we have from *Tebleb,* viz. *The chief and principal men among the Arabians, when the night is fo dark that their tents cannot be feen by travellers, choofe the mountain or hill that is neareft to them, where they kindle a fire, and give particular charge to have it kept up, till the morning, as a place of retirement for night-travellers.* Vid. *Anthol. vet.* ed. *Schult.* p. 473. and *Carm. Togr.* v. 23. and Note on *Kailanenfis,* p. 58.

Pag. 74. *The courfe: Midmáron:* properly fignifies the fpace of forty days, in which a horfe is fed more liberally, that he may grow fat, and after this return to his ufual allowance, that his fatnefs may wear off, and he may appear outwardly thinner and flenderer. Such an horfe is called *modámmiron, reduced to his old fhape.* The *hippodromus,* or place for *race-horfes horſes*, is likewiſe named *midmáron*, and applied by the Arabians to the *race of virtue: of eloquence: of munificence: of courage: of death.*

Ib. *Watchers:* From hence we learn that the Mahometans, in imitation of the Jews, appointed men to *watch* and give notice of the firſt appearance of the moon.

Ib. *The day*, &c. Arab. *Till the day was worn out with old age:* or, *till it waxed decrepid and expired:* a phraſe common to Greeks and Latins, who ſpeak of the *Spring* as being *young, adult,* and *growing old.* The ſame figure is applied to *praiſe,* to *fame,* to *fortune,* &c. *jamque multa edita ſtrage pugna feneſcebat. Liv.* l. 4.

Ib. *The light*, &c. Arab. *The edge or border of the day was falling,* or *ſinking* to the weſt. *Præceps in 'veſperam dies.*

Ib. *Sun darkened.* Arab. *The ſun appeared in his ragged garments,* viz. When the radiant veil of night, with which he was clothed, by the darkneſs that gradually increaſed, was changed to a tattered, ſordid, ſackcloth-robe. Comp. *Rev.* vi. 12. *The ſun became black as ſackcloth of hair,* viz. When obſcured by black clouds.

Ib. *Outward behaviour*, &c. Arab. *Who appeared outwardly a verdant herb; but within a mere dung-hill:* proverbially applied to thoſe who *make fair and large promiſes, without any intention to perform them.* One of *Mahomet*'s ſayings, by tradition, is, *Beware of the verdant outſide of dung.* And being aſked what he meant by it; replied, *A beautiful young woman ſprung from evil parents.* Our author *Hariri* in another place ſpeaks in the ſame figure, viz. *The verdure of his dung deceived me ſo far as to make me enter into his familiar acquaintance.* i. e. *His ſeeming-honeſt, liberal behaviour,* &c.

Pag. 75. *Fabulous account. Al-Churáphah: a word,* *Tebleb* obſerves, *in every body's mouth,* proverbially *applied to all inſignificant diſcourſe, and in which there is no truth: Such diſcourſe, Abulbeka writes, as occaſions admiration and laughter: looſe and inconſiſtent, like fruit,*

7

which

which *churipha, is cut, and divided* into feveral parts. From hence *charáph,* denotes *weaknefs of mind,* and *al-charíph, a perfon of that ftamp.*   Others derive it from one whofe name was *Churápha,* who was feized by *Genii,* [or *Dæmons,* vid. *Alcor.* vi. v. 128] and making his efcape from them, related feveral ftrange ftories concerning what had happened to him.

Ib. *Make an atonement, &c.* Arab. *Teawwadhow.* Literally, *Confugerunt,* viz. ad Deum averruncum. i. e. They appealed to God in their behalf. *Maádhallábi: Confugium Dei.*   And *Aówdho ila-'llábi: confugio ad Deum,* are folemn proteftations frequently ufed by the Arabians: to avert any divine judgement: the fame with, *avertat Deus!*

ASSEMBLY V.

ENTITLED

C U F E N S I S.

THE narrative which *Harith* the fon of *Hemmam* gives of himfelf, is as follows. Once in my travels, when the night to the eye appeared as it were with a clothing of different colours, occafioned by the moon's fhining with a mixture of light and darknefs; which in comparifon you might refemble to a filver *amulet*; I happened at *Cufa* to enter into converfation with a fociety of men, *verfed* in the politeft arts of eloquence: to fuch a degree that even *Sebban* himfelf could not be compared to them. Upon what fubject foever they difcourfed, that which they alledged was fo profitable and worthy of remembrance; that there was no one, who gave the leaft due attention, but muft receive confiderable advantage from it. So clear, and free, and innocent, that there was no neceffity for any caution to be given, no fear of any bad confequence arifing from it. In fhort, fo very entertaining, that inftead of creating jealoufy in the audience, it engaged them to enter into the ftricteft bonds of unanimity and friendfhip. This night-converfation affected us to fuch a degree, that there was no poffibility of withdrawing from it, till the light of the moon difappeared, and we were forced to fubmit to the power of fleep, notwithftanding the moft refolute ftruggles to fupport our vigilance. And no fooner had the *night* fpread it's veil of the thickeft darknefs, and a general nodding and flumbering prevailed, but from the gate we heard a low, mur-

murring

muring voice, in found refembling the *barking of a
dog* ; which was followed foon after by a loud knock-
ing at the door, eagerly requefting that it might be
opened. To whom we faid, What ftranger is this ?
what misfortune hath happened to him, that he
fhould travel in fo very dark a night, and make this
a place of refuge ? To which he gave this anfwer :

> *May happinefs this family attend,*
> *From the calamities of life fecure !*
> *Your days furviving, may you all enjoy,*
> *Guarded from injuries of ev'ry kind !*
> *Compell'd by darknefs fpreading o'er the night,*
> *[Clouds fly on clouds in thickeft union join'd,]*
> *A fqualid traveller, with duft befmear'd,*
> *Begs for refrefhment from your bounteous dome.*
> *To tedious motions deftin'd is my life.*
> *Thefe with much toil and labour I purfue.*
> *The hardfhips I endure, pow'rful and ftrong,*
> *Make me an objet of uncommon form.*
> *I'm fo contracted that my head and feet,*
> *Their pofture change, almoft in union join:*
> *My vifage pale, like th' horizontal moon,*
> *When fcarce three days are number'd to her age.*
> *In my diftrefs'd condition I prefume*
> *An humble fupplicant t' approach your court.*
> *No perfons in the univerfe fo well difpos'd,*
> *Petitions from poor objets to receive !*
> *Some tokens of your hofpitality*
> *An indigent petitioner requefts.*
> *Your kind reception, tho' your bounty's fmall,*
> *Will foon difcover my contented mind.*
> *To ev'ry change adapted is my tafte :*
> *For fweet or bitter I am well prepared.*
> *So far from filence ! in the ftrongeft terms*
> *With praife your gen'rous acts I'll celebrate.*

After this incident, *Harith Ibn Hemmam* thus continues his narrative. When by the harmony and
fweetnefs of his poetry he had engaged our affections to fuch a degree, that even our very heart was
pierced and wounded ; and when we thoroughly un-

derftood

derftood *what power* of eloquence he was poffeffed of, which flowed from him like fo many fudden fhowers of rain from the clouds ; to prevent any more folicitation we made all the difpatch that was poffible to open the gate, and to receive him with the tendereft expreffions of congratulation : calling aloud to the young man who attended us, Make hafte, make hafte, without the leaft delay, and bring what provifion you find is the readieft to be had. But the ftranger protefted by him who *conducted* me to your manfion, I am determined not *to tafte any of your hofpitable provifion*, unlefs you abfolutely promife that you will give yourfelves no extraordinary trouble on my account, and not imagine you are under any ne-ceffity of eating any thing, purely to oblige me, at this unfeafonable juncture. For to load the ftomach by *frequent eating*, is the occafion of much crudity and choler : we are therefore by an *interdict* forbid to indulge the appetite. And in my opinion, he muft be efteemed the moft unwelcome ftranger, who gives trouble and difturbance to a family, that favours him with a kind and generous reception : efpecially when there arifes from it any injury to the body, and a foundation is laid for feveral kinds of ficknefles and difeafes. We muft not wonder then at that common proverb, *The beft fupper we eat, is by day-light.* The proper, and indeed the only meaning of which is, to be quick in difpatching our evening repaft, and to avoid regaling ourfelves in the night with fuch food, that fo far from affording due nourifhment, it pro-duces weaknefs in the eyes, and dimnefs in our fight. What you obferve, I proteft, is much to the purpofe, only with this exception ; *unlefs one's hunger increafes to excefs ;* and if not fatisfied, we can enjoy no eafe, nor reft. The obfervation that *Harith* made, was, His whole behaviour was fuch as if he was refolved to know the intimate fecrets of our mind, and thorough-ly *underftand which way our inclination directed us.* Therefore without any hefitation we treated him in the moft obliging manner, gratifying his requeft,

agreeing

agreeing to the condition he propofed ; and expreffing ourfelves largely in commendation of that *difpofition of mind*, in which nature had formed him. When
the waiter brought what repaft was the readieft to be
got, and had lighted a candle, fo as that we could
diftinguifh one perfon from another, I fixed my eyes
intenfly on the man, and who fhould he be but *Abuzeid ?* I then fpoke to my companions ; congratulating them on the reception of fo confiderable a ftranger, or rather, fo *rich a fpoil.* To this name he is
juftly intitled ; for though the heavens are now covered with darknefs, and that *remarkable ftar* is fet ;
yet to make us amends *the ftar of poetry rifes.* And
though the fplendor of the moon hath fecreted and
concealed itfelf in the night ; yet we receive abun-
dant fatisfaction from the *light* of that elegant *profe-
language* with which we are entertained. The reflection
that a perfon of fuch extraordinary accomplifhments
had favoured them with his prefence, raifed in them
an inexpreffible fervency of joy ; and SLEEP, to whofe
power their eyes had fubmitted, took her flight as
fwift as the motion of a bird. As to the eafe and reft
which they were prepared to enjoy, they now entirely *abandoned* it ; and *refumed* with much pleafure
their humorous converfation, which for fome time
had been filenced. *Abuzeid* in the mean while employed his hands as quick as poffible in the work he
was engaged, till the whole mefs they had fet before
him was entirely confumed ; and he fignified to the
company that the table, there being no farther occafion for it, might be taken away. We then made our
requeft to him, that he would entertain us with a
fpecimen of fome new hiftory, fome of his curious
and uncommon night-difcourfes : or fuch expeditions
as he had met with in his travels, which might appear
to us in an unufual and extraordinary light. To which
he replied, By experience I can truly fay, that of all
the wonderful events which men either as fpectators
have feen, or have related as hiftorians ; there is one
thing very remarkable hath happened, to which this

very

very night mine eyes were witness, a little before I made my address to you, and presumed to knock at your gates. We were then very solicitous in desiring he would give us a narrative of the strange adventure which this night's-travel had produced. To this he answered; My motions have been such, that I may compare them to the swift uncertain passage of an arrow, darted from the bow without any particular direction. These motions have brought me as an exile to this country, labouring under extreme want and poverty; miserable to the highest degree; *my money totally exhausted.* But instead of desponding and sinking under my burden, I determined to take my course, even in the silent night, when the heavens were involved *in darkness.* My feet for want of shoes so tender and bruised, that I was scarce able to tread the ground! my intention was to find out, if possible, an hospitable person, who would supply me with provision: or by my own management, by some means or other, to procure, if it was but a cake or morsel of bread, to satisfy my craving appetite. But not succeeding in my projects, HUNGER, like a camel-driver, hath made me wander from one circuit to another; and FATE, who delights in sporting with wondrous events, [and for that reason justly entitled the *parent of miracles*] with their united strength have forced me from place to place, till at last I took up my rest at the gate of some person, though quite a stranger to me : where I recited the following verses :

> *Hail! to this hospitable mansion, hail !*
> *May the inhabitants with lib'ral hand*
> *Diffuse their bounteous store, like tender plants,*
> *From which distills constant, refreshing juice.*
> *Behold a* traveller in great distress!
> *Fatigu'd and hungry, begs your present aid :*
> *Like* meager, *pur-blind* camel, *in the night,*
> *Beating the ground thro' strange, uncertain paths.*
> *His bowels raging with an ardent flame ;*
> *Contracted for the want of common food,*

During

During the courſe of two long tedious days,
No ſingle morſel for his eager taſte!
Travers'd your country, tho' in diff'rent parts,
And yet no comfortable refuge find.
In thickeſt darkneſs all the earth's involv'd,
Spreading *around it's melancholy ſhade.*
Thus here in much aſtoniſhment I ſtand,
Parch'd like the bread on red-hot embers plac'd:
Or to the ſick man's feueriſh complaint,
M' uneaſy, reſtleſs motions I compare.
Is this the manſion of a gen'rous ſoul,
Where wearied pilgrims for refreſhment hope?
Let me from hence the pleaſing voice receive:
Throw down thy ſtaff, *enter without reſtraint.*
Chearful thy countenance, do thou appear
With ev'ry mark of hoſpitable joy.

Having repeated theſe verſes, the firſt perſon that
preſented himſelf to me, was a little young man,
(who might be compared to a young ſtag, or a wild
calf brought up in the woods) clothed in a linen garment, and thus addreſſed himſelf to me:

By venerable Abraham I ſwear,
Parent of friendly hoſpitality:
The great reſtorer of that ſacred dome,
Which beautifies the world's metropolis;
To which religious pilgrims have reſort
From diſtant climes to pay their ſolemn vows.
When an unfortunate night-traveller
In great diſtreſs petitions our relief,
No other aid, but freely to converſe,
Muſt he expect, and for his camels reſt.
For entertainment how ſhall he prepare,
Whoſe eyes are dim for want of uſual ſleep?
A rav'nous ſtranger how ſhall be ſupply,
Whoſe very bones through meager fleſh appear?
If my words deviate from the rules of truth,
To thy impartial judgement I ſubmit.

To this I replied, What ſhall I do? What refreſhment am I to hope for in a deſolate manſion, provid-
ed

ed with neither food nor drink? and what have I to
expect from a perſon ſo very neceſſitous, that without
any impropriety one may call him *Poverty's affociate.*
But pray, young man, give me leave to aſk the favour of your name? for I muſt confeſs, the natural
genius and diſpoſition you ſeem to be poſſeſſed of,
makes ſuch an impreſſion as to affect me with an unaccountable paſſion of uneaſineſs. He, without the
leaſt heſitation, anſwered, My name is *Zeido*, and
Pheida is my native country. It is but a little while
ago ſince I came into theſe parts, accompanied with
my uncles, whoſe family is deſcended from thoſe of
Ebſis. On his mentioning this, I was very importunate to hear ſome farther account concerning him,
applying the common *form* of ſpeech, *May thy life
be preſerved ſo as to be reſtored.* He then immediately proceeded in his narration, and in order to give
me more particulars relating to himſelf, he proceeded
in this manner. My mother *Berra*, a name that intimates her pious and religious diſpoſition, gave me
this hiſtory : *viz.* That in the remarkable year when
Mawána was taken and ravaged by the enemy, ſhe
was married to a man of note and diſtinguiſhed character, deſcended from the principal family of *Serugium* and *Gaſſan*. But as ſoon as he perceived ſhe
was with child, having by common fame the character of one whoſe pleaſure was to travel from one
diſtant part of the world to another, he took an opportunity of privately withdrawing himſelf from her,
without acquainting her with his intention. From that
time we are entirely ignorant what is become of him ;
whether he is ſtill alive, ſo as that we may have any
farther expectation of ſeeing him ; or whether he hath
made his grave in ſome ſolitary deſert. Theſe particular circumſtances were no ſooner mentioned, than
they appeared to me, ſaid *Abuzeid*, ſo clear, ſo ſtrong
and evident, that of a certainty I concluded, this
muſt be my ſon. But the mean and deſpicable figure
I made, (occaſioned by the want of proviſions, to
ſuch a degree, that like an empty veſſel you might hear
the

the wind, as it were, whisper through me) discouraged
me from making myself known to him. For this
reason, in opposition to the tenderness of fatherly affection, I forcibly withdrew myself; though at the
same time the disorder that I suffered was such, that
every part within me was much injured, and mine
eyes discharged even floods of tears. Tell me now,
you that are my hearty, sincere friends, did you ever
hear any thing more strange and unaccountable than
this ? The answer we made was with this asseveration :
*No ; by him in whose possession is the knowledge of the
book !* If this is the case, let me desire you to enter it
as such into the *book of wonderful events :* And that it
may not be forgot, but transmitted to everlasting memory, let it be inserted in the *middle of the pages of
that book :* for no part in the universe is able to produce an instance of any history parallel to it. And
having ordered an inkhorn with proper instruments
to be brought, we committed to writing the whole
narrative in the same manner, and in the same con-
nection as it was reported. The next question we
asked him, was, What his real sentiments were in regard to his son, whether he was desirous of taking
him under his immediate protection? To which he replied, When *my circumstances* are in a happier condition than they are at present, I shall then be better
qualified to discharge the duty of a father, and to be
his defence and protection. We then said to him, if
any reasonable sum of money would satisfy thee, we
are ready to make a collection immediately. Strange
indeed! he replied, should I not be easy and contented with any part of the bounty you are pleased to
favour me with. But was it really of less value than
what you intend, no one in his senses should refuse
or despise it. Therefore every one of us judged it ne-
cessary to make the distribution, to put down in
writing the sum we proposed for him ; and oblige
ourselves as strictly to pay it, as if we had given him
our bill or bond. This was so pleasing to him, that
his gratitude was raised to a very high degree, ex-
pressing

preffing his obligation with all the encomiums imaginable, and fetting forth our generous benefaction
in the fulleft and moft magnificent terms : in terms
fo large and copious, that his words were rather tedious and too prolix ; for we really did not think the
kindnefs we had fhewn him deferved fuch commendations. The *difcourfe* that he delivered after this was
fo elegant and entertaining, adorned with all the
flowers of eloquence, fet off with fuch a beautiful variety of language ; that were you to compare it with
the rich and fplendid garments of *jemama*, fo curioufly
wrought, and mixed with fuch numbers of pleafing
colours ; thefe were fo far from being equal to it, that
they muft appear to your eye but very mean and
contemptible. This difcourfe he continued till the
rays of the fun appeared, and the morning began to
fpread. Our night was fpent with fo much eafe and
pleafure, as to be free from all kind of interruption
whatfoever, even till the *light* itfelf was *vifible:* fo
agreeable was the converfation which engaged us,
before that *Harbinger* of the morning had prefented
himfelf. No fooner had the *rays of the fun* difperfed
themfelves, but *with a motion* fwift as that of a doe,
he ftarted up, and faid, Come, imitate the birds, and
rife up quickly, that we may collect the prefents of
our benefactors, fo as to be fatisfied what fums of
money we fhall poffefs, which we have now the promife of. For indeed I muft confefs to you, *Every
part belonging to me is in much diforder* on account of
my fon, through that tender love and affection that
I bear towards him. Then I *took him by the hand,*
and did not let it go till I had difpatched the affair
I was engaged in. But having gathered up the money, and put it into his purfe, the lines of his forehead fparkled, and fhined like a glittering fword, or
a bright cloud: by which he fignified the tranfports
of his joy ; expreffing himfelf in thefe words : "May
thy reward be *equal to the merit* of thy actions ! and
my earneft requeft to God, is, that *he would* be pleafed *to repay* thee this kindnefs, which of myfelf I am

not

not able to do." To which I anfwered, My great defire is, to be one of thy companions in travel; the
reafon I have for this requeft is, that I may have the
pleafure of enjoying not only the prefence, but the
agreeable converfation of thy fon, a youth endowed
with the moft excellent, and amiable qualities. Having requefted of him this favour, he looked upon
me in the fame manner, and with the fame countenance, as a deceiver looks upon the man he hath deceived: and burfting out into a laughter, fo loud,
and fo fudden, that his eyes were *full of tears*; he
gave me this fpecimen of his poetical genius:

The fun, when rais'd to his meridian height,
Gives thee a profpect of fome wat'ry clouds,
That on the furface of the earth are mov'd.
But 'tis a vapour only, thou 'rt deceiv'd.
With fuch delufion *my difcourfe compare.*
In terms fo obvious was my art conceal'd;
In words fo plain and clear my doubts exprefs'd;
That not the leaft fufpicion made me think
Their real meaning could be mifapplied.
By the Supreme of heaven and earth I fwear,
I am depriv'd of Berra's *tender love.*
Of proper iffue I am deftitute;
No fon to take the furname *I would give.*
But yet I muft, I cannot but confefs,
That ftratagems from my invention form'd,
Of various fcenes, of different degrees,
Have been th' employment of my bufy life:
Not unpremeditated, but produc'd
From all the efforts of my art and fkill.
Such as the NARRATIVES *of* Afmaceus,
With his ftrong ornaments of beauteous profe,
Did never fhew, nor the poetic vein,
That flow'd fo fweetly in Cumeithus's *ftyle.*
Thefe arts of fubtilty, of fo much ufe,
As ready inftruments of frefh fupply
To ev'ry changing incident of time,
With th' utmoft care I've labour'd to preferve.

Should

Should I defert thefe neceffary aids ;
Were all my actions pure and innocent ;
My ftate of life ! how great would be the change!
How deftitute of what I now poffefs !
But if I've fpoke with language not reftrain'd ;
If criminal my liberty of fpeech ;
The favour of excufe I muft defire ;
Your kind forgivenefs is my ftrong requeft.

He then bid me farewell; but not without *leav-ing* fuch an impreffion on my heart, as muft of neceffity continue for a long time before it could be removed.

NOTES

NOTES

ON

ASSEMBLY V.

ENTITLED

CUFENSIS.

PAG. 86. *Amulet: tawidhon: a piece of silver* [according to *Tebleb*'s defcription] *made round like the moon, part of the circle being hollow, as an iron horfe-fhoe. This is tied by a thread, and faftened to children's necks by way of charm. Some have an infcription on them.* Vid. Not. on *Affemb.* IV. ult.

Ib. *Cufa:* A city of Babylonian *Irak*, or *Erak*, which *Seleucus*, furnamed *Nicator*, poffeffed after the death of *Alexander*. Vid. *Greg. Ab. Phar. Dynaft.* p. 98, and 188.

Ib. *Verfed,* &c. Arab. *Nurfed with the milk of eloquence.*

Ib. *Sebban,* &c. Arab. *They drew the cloak of oblivion over Sebban himfelf. Sebban,* rather *Sebban Wail,* was efteemed the moft eloquent of the Arabians: from whence they fay of a learned eloquent man, proverbially, *He draws the cloak,* &c. i. e. When he fpeaks, we muft blot out the memory of *Sebban.* To wear a long robe hanging down to the ancles denotes pomp and magnificence. Vid. *Affembly* the IVth, at the beginning, where the higheft profperity is expreffed by long garments: confequently, *to wear the robe of eloquence,* is expreffive of a great orator.

Pag. 87. *Barking of a dog:* Which *Tebleb* explains from a perfon's travelling in the night, and not knowing

G
ing

ing what diftance he is from any place of reception, imitates the *barking of a dog*; and if near enough to be heard, the dogs return the found. Thither he retires for his night's accommodation.

Ib. *Tedious*, &c. Arab. *I am the brother of travel.* i. e. I am a conftant traveller. *The brother of any thing*, *Tebleb* faith, is that to which any one gives ftrict attendance.

Ib. *Horizontal moon*, not quite three days old, is called *hilálon*: all the reft of its time, *kámaron*. The verb applied to her when young, is, *iftárra*, *fhines but little*: fo as to let you know her age. From hence the proverb, *His eye*, *firárobo*, *is his difcoverer*. i. e. By his afpect only you know what is in him. The comparifon of our Poet here is very elegant: *Abuzeid*, grown pale and crooked, refembles himfelf to the moon, when it firft appears.

Pag. 88. *What power*, &c. Arab. *What force or efficacy was concealed behind his thunder.* A truly learned man, qualified to teach and inftruct others, is compared to a cloud that difcharges plenteous fhowers to moiften and make the earth fruitful: not like an empty cloud that burfts with thunder, but produces no rain. Vid. Not. on *Affembly* II. p. 40.

Ib. *Conducted me*, *abálla-ni*. The fubftantive of which is, an *inn*, or place for the reception of ftrangers. From hence the Arabians fay, fpeaking of human infirmity, *al-infáno mahállo nifyáni: Man is the inn, or feat of oblivion.*

Ib. *Tafte of*, &c. *La telammátto: non circumlambam: I will not roll*, or *ufe my tongue*, to tafte any of your provifions. And by a metaphor, *to roll a queftion about the tongue*, is, *to exercife it fo as to have it always prepared for a lye.*

Ib. *Frequent, eating.* The Arabians fay, *To be frequently eating hinders one's eating.*

Ib. *Interdict húrrámat: interdicit quafi facrum:* a word elegantly applied here to moderation in eating, as a matter of *facred and religious concern.*

Ib. *Beſt ſupper*, &c. *Ibn Doreid* in an humourous manner, writes,

I ſee, *al-iſká, dimneſs*, in the eye,
Appear frequently *min-al-aſhai, after ſupper*.

Ib. *One's hunger*, &c. Arab: *Unleſs the fire of hunger burns to a great degree.*

———————— *Furit ardor edendi*
Perque avidas fauces, immenſaque viſcera regnat.
                                Ovid. Metam. 8.

Ib. *Underſtand*, &c. Arab. *To throw the dart at our mind from the bow* [*kidátina*] *of our purpoſe, or intention.* i. e. To know how we ſtood affected. *Kidáton* is a word applied by the Mahometans to *an orthodox faith.* An heretic, they ſay, *does not dart from the bow of faith:* and he who does ſo, is ſpoken of as agreeing with you both in religious and civil concerns.

Pag. 89. *Diſpoſition of mind.* Arab. *Cholokon* : A temper *poliſhed*, from *chálaka, to form*, or *ſhape. A great genius, formed for every virtue*, is expreſſed by *chólokon adímon : Alcor.* c. lxviii. 5. To *chólokon* our Author adds *ſabtin*, elegantly comparing a good diſpoſition to what is *ſtraight and even.* From hence the Arabians ſay, a generous man is *ſabton, ſtraight* in his hands : i. e. His hand is always ſtretched out to ſhew his liberality. On the contrary, a covetous churl has *crooked hands or fingers :* i. e. He is ſo cloſe-fiſted, that he will not open his hand for any charitable purpoſe.

Ib. *Rich a ſpoil* : What the Arabians call *al-mágnamo-'lbárido : præda frigida :* A ſpoil that is gained without oppoſition, taken in war without any engagement, or the loſs of blood.

Ib. *Remarkable ſtar : Kámaro-'ſhira : luna Sirii*, viz: *Luna quæ Sirio vicina eſt : The ſtar of poetry : Kámaro-'ſhiri : luna carminis : The poetical ſtar, viz. Abu-zeid.* You obſerve here the *paronomoſia*, too tenaciouſly affected by the Arabian Poets.

Ib. *Light of proſe language :* The Author continues his figurative expreſſions, as if *Abu-zeid's* common

diſcourſe

difcourfe was fo excellent, as to want no luminary to recommend it: and as the moon gives light to a dark night, fo does his language to a clouded underftanding.

Ib: *Abandoned, &c. Ráfadow.* The force of which word implies, *They let it take it's own courfe, like camels that are permitted to wander without reftraint.*

Ib. *Refumed, &c.* The Arab: literally is, *That humourous converfation which they had fhut up, they again unfolded.* A phrafe applied to the freedom of difcourfe, refembling thofe Eaftern tapeftry carpets, when expanded and fpread out: in oppofition to narrow and contracted language, compared to carpets rolled up and folded. Thus we read in the hiftory of *Timur,* expreffed in the fublime Eaftern ftyle, " The hangings of the fecrets being removed, or, *Tamerlan,* by *Ahmed Ben Arabfiades,* publifhed in *Arabic* by *Golius,* p. 9. *Imtáddo lilbáfti bifáton: The carpet* was fpread *for familiar converfation.*" P. 256, " On a day of publick rejoicing, *he folded,* or *fhut up the carpet* of whatever might obftruct their joy, and *expanded,* or *fpread the carpet* of wine and mufic." P. 197, " They fpread the *carpet of difcourfe*: i. e. Their difcourfe was free and open." P. 421, " He folded up the *carpet of humanity*: i. e. His behaviour was rough and churlifh." The Arabians fay proverbially, *Love, when folded, continues longer than when expanded:* the fame with, *Too much familiarity breeds contempt.*

Pag. 90. *My money, &c.* Arab. *My purfe refembles the heart of Mofes's mother.* A proverbial expreffion, alluding to a paffage in the *Alcoran,* ch. xxviii. 10. where it is mentioned, when *Pharaob* was difputing whether he fhould kill *Mofes,* and was diffuaded from it, " The heart of Mofes's mother became *phárigan, vacuum.* Which fome interpret to a good fenfe, as *free from trouble and anxiety.* Others, to a bad one, viz. *void,* or *empty, through fear and ftupor, even to defpair.* This latter fenfe *Hariri* applies to himfelf, as defpairing of relief.

Ib.

Ib. *Darkness: Dójan :* Such as *covers* or *involves the night in great obscurity.* The Mahometans apply this word to their religion : as if it was fo extenfive, that by way of proverb, they fay, *Dája-'l-iflámo cólla fháiin: cooperuit omnia iflamifmus :. It prevails fo much as to meet with no obftruction.*

Ib. *Traveller.* Arab. *Son of a journey,* or, *the way :* [vid. *Ch. Comt.* on *Job v.* 7.] fo called, as *Tebleb* writes, *Becaufe people have no other knowledge of him, than that he is a traveller. Terræ filius,* among the Latins, bears the fame character. To this purpofe is the Arabian *Ænigma ;* intimating that he whofe life is fpent in continually moving from one place to another, is not able to give an account of his birth or parents from whence he defcended, viz.

> *By revelation in the Alcoran,*
> *An unbegotten race of men we find :*
> *Some that are very far advanc'd in years :*
> *Others adorn'd with all the bloom of youth.*

Ib. *In great diftrefs, mórmilon : reduced to a fand.* i. e. So deftitute of provifions, that he hath not a morfel left fo big as a fand. From hence *Tebleb,* according to *Abulbeka,* obferves, that a man who hath loft his wife, is called *armal :* and a woman that has loft her hufband, *armalat :* being by fuch lofs reduced to poverty.

Ib. *Meager camel : nídwon.* Fatigued with travelling, fo as to be all in rags.

Ib. *In the night :* Arab. *Beating the ground with his feet, like a camel in the night, not knowing which way to move.* From hence the proverb : *As the pur-blind camel beats the ground.* Applied to a perfon bewildered in the night, and in wrath beating the ground with his feet, uncertain which way to fteer his courfe. *In the night,* is exprefs'd in Arab. by an adjective formed from the fubftantive, viz. *Lailon ályalo : nox noctofiffima.* Thus we read, *Rom.* vii. 13. καθ' υπερβολην αμαρτωλος η αμαρτια: *fin exceeding finful.*

G 3   Pag.

Pag. 91. *Spreading*, &c. The Arabic here very beautifully compares *darkness* to a *bird* letting down it's wings hovering over the earth. The original ex-presses it by *the wing of darkness inclining*. From hence the Poet in *Hamasa*:

> *The night appears extremely dark,*
> *When both her feather'd wings hang down.*

· Ib. *The mansion*, &c. Arab. *In this house is there a receptacle of sweet water?* i. e. " Is there here a man of so much liberality and munificence, possessed of sweet waters for such as seek refreshment ?"

Ib. *Throw down thy staff.* Applied *to one who finds rest in his travels:* and to him *whose affairs are regulated and well disposed. Mild with his staff,* is the same as *administring justice in mercy:* or, *as a shepherd who gently drives his flock.* On the contrary, *weak in his staff,* he *who takes but little care of them. Cruel with his staff,* denotes *a rigid governor,* or *tyrant. Splitting of the staff,* is *discord. Breaking it,* the *casting away of care. To depart from true religion,* is, *to break it's staff. To break the staff of Moslemen,* is, *to separate from them.*

· Ib. *By venerable Abraham.* Arab. *By the reverence of al-shaich: the old man:* Abraham emphatically so called, though a name given not only to men advanced in age, but to such as are distinguished by their learn-ing, power, piety, &c.

˗ Ib. *Sacred dome,* or temple of *Mecca*; which by our Poet is entitled *metropolis of the world.* The Ma-hometans have a tradition that this temple was built several ages before *Mahomet.* Some say it was destroyed by the flood : others, that it was carried up to heaven during the flood ; was restored by Abraham, and pre-served to the time of *Mahomet.* Vid. *Alcor.* ch. ii. v. 128. Edit. *Marrac. Dav. Mill. Dissert.* 10. §. 11. *Sale's Prelim. Disc.* to translation of *Cor.* p. 114.

Ib. *Whose bones,* &c. Arab. His bones for want of flesh appear as if *ánbora, he was chipped with an hatchet.* I gave the bow to *Barijáha: it's hewer;* is

a proa proverb, viz. *I reſtored the goods to their right owner.* The Arabians, ſpeaking of an old man whoſe troubles are multiplied, ſay, " Troubles *have hewed him.*" The ſame phraſe they apply to calamities of any kind. For inſtance, " Misfortunes and time *have hewed his hair :*" i. e. Have waſted his plenteous fortunes, and left him none of his thick and well-compacted plumes remaining.

Pag. 92. *Pheida :* A town ſituated between *Mecca* and *Bagdad.*

Ib. *Form,* viz. *Iſhta wa-noíſhta : Live and be reſtored :* of the ſame force with what the Arabians ſay, *Naúſhca-l-láho : God raiſe thee up,* viz. from thy poverty to a happier ſtate !

Ib. *Mawána :* A place, or as others, a town in the way to *Mecca. Serugium :* Vid. Not. ult. on *Aſſemb.* I. *Gaſſan :* Vid. Not. p. 32. on *Aſſemb.* II.

Pag. 93. *The book,* &c. He is ſuppoſed to refer either to the *Alcoran,* or *the table of God's decrees.* Vid. *Alcor.* ch. vi. v. 37. viz. *Ma farátna fi-'l-citábi,* &c. *We have omitted* nothing *in the book :* i. e. *In the preſerved table,* in which is recorded whatever hath or ſhall come to paſs in the world. Abſolute predeſtination with regard to this preſent as well as future life being the doctrine of Mahometans in the ſtricteſt ſenſe : a doctrine that *Mahomet* made great uſe of in his ſurprizing conqueſts. Vid. *Sale's Prelim. Diſc.* to *Cor.* p. 64 and 103.

Ib. *Wonderful events :* Referring, it is ſuppoſed, to a book with *that title.*

Ib. *In the middle,* &c. Arab. *In ventribus* [*awrákin*] *foliorum : In the middle of thoſe leaves* or *pages :* alluding to the cuſtom of writing on *leaves of trees,* before the invention of *paper. Wárakon,* the ſingular of *awrákon,* ſignifying a *leaf* and *paper.* Both which the Poet *Nawabig* includes in theſe verſes :

No fruit that ripens when [*wárakon*] *the leaf* is green,
With greater beauty to the eye appears,
Than th' Author's ſtile, with utmoſt pleaſure read,
When on white [*wárakon*] *paper* carefully inſcrib'd.

Ib.

Ib. *My circumstances*, &c. Arab. *When the sleeve of my garment is heavier, the education of my son will be lighter.* *His back is heavy loaden*, and on the contrary, *his burden is light*; are phrases, intimating either a person's *numerous family*, or, *his small number of domestics.*

Ib. *Writing: Kitton: A libel*, or *declaration in law of a debt that is contracted. The sentence of a Judge: an instrument of donation.* *Alcor.* ch. xxxviii. v. 17. Hasten *kittána*, *our sentence*, or *portion*, before the day of account: i. e. The day of judgement.

Pag. 94. *Discourse.* The Arabic here compares his language to a beautiful picture; but yet far exceeding all the art of the Painter. So ornamental, that the inhabitants of *Jemáma*, remarkable for making the most curious and variegated garments, were not equal to him.

Ib. *Jemáma*, strictly speaking, is, *Arabia Felix*, being the best and finest of those five parts, into which the whole country is divided. Vid. *Geograph. Index to the life of Saladin*, by *Schultens.*

Ib. *Light visible.* Arab. *Till the black hairs of the night waxed white.* ··

Ib. *Harbinger*, &c. Arab. *The column of the morning broke forth.* ··

Ib. *Rays of the sun.* Arab. *Horn of the fawn.* A phrase in the East, signifying the *rising of the sun.* *Horn* being the same with *radiant light:* because, say the Arabians, *As rays dart from the heavens*, so does the bright colour *of* does shine from the tops of mountains. A *doe* is one of the names they ascribe to the sun. Thus the Poet:

The Doe that shines with brightest rays
T' illuminate the day;
Is much inferior to the charms
Of Female's beauteous face.
For she with all her splendor sets
In dark obscurity:
But this appears without eclipse,
By day and night the same.

Vid. Not. on *Traveller*, v. 29.

The

The nofe of the fun fneezed to me ; is proverbially applied to *the appearance of the morning*, or the *rifing of
the fun.* From what is premifed, confider the *title* to
Pfal. xxii. viz. *Aijéleth ha-fhachar : cerva matutina : the
morning-hind :* compared with *Cantic.* viii. ult. " Make
hafte, my beloved, and be thou like to *a roe*, or to *a
young hart* upon the mountains of fpices."

. Ib. *With a motion*, &c. Arab. *He danced the dance
of a doe.*

Ib. *Every part*, &c. Arab. *My liver* (my inward
parts) *are all on a float, founding within me in the fame
manner with that noife which a Female makes in her
throat on account of her young.*

Ib. *Took him by the hand.* Arab. *I join'd my fide*, or,
rather, *my wing to his :* the fame as, *I went with him
hand in hand.* The *wing* and *the hand*, being fynoni-
mous terms.

Ib. *Equal to*, &c. Arab. May thy reward be equal
to the motions *kadamica, of thy feet.* He who moves
towards another, *with a right foot*, is equivalent to
one who treats him *with a virtuous and ingenuous
mind. Sure footed*, intimates a man of *fkill and underftanding :* and a friend *of long continuance.*

Ib. *That God would repay.* Arab. That he would
be my *chálipha, vicar*, or *fucceffor.* From hence the
Arabians, by way of confolation to a perfon in diftrefs,
fay, May God be to thee *chálipha, vicarius*, inftead of
a father !

Pag. 95. *Full of tears : Tegárgerat : gargarizavit
uterque oculus :* i. e. His eyes flowing with tears, made
the fame noife with that of a *gargarifm*, when you
gargle the mouth or throat.

Ib. *Watery clouds : Sárabon.* A fpecies of water
that at noon-day appears in barren, fandy fields, as if
it was real water ; but foon paffes away as a vapour
only.

Ib. *With fuch delufion*, &c. Arab. *Rawaíto : I have
propofed*, literally, *watered* my difcourfe. He aims at
the profpect of *faráb, the appearance of water*, is an
adagy, fignifying the folly of one who is fatisfied
with

with the outward fhew of a thing, and not entering
into the merit of it   Compare *Ifai.* xxxv. 7. *ba-
fhatab: the parched ground* fhall become a pool.   A
fhew, or appearance of water in the defert, invites a
thirfty traveller; but coming near it, he is fenfible of
his error; for it foon vanifhes away.   To this failure
are refembled the tranfitory affairs of the world; which
however plaufible and engaging in profpect, the event
difcovers the vanity of our imagination.   Vid. *Adag.
Arab.* 55. *Gol.* ed.

Ib. *Berra:* Signifies *a beneficent, kind mother.*

Ib. *Surname: Iltanaîto: cui cognomen dare poffum:*
it being ufual with the Arabians to add a name to
their fons befides that of their fathers.   Vid. *Pref.* to
the *Traveller.*   From the fame radix, viz. *cána,* is
cóxwaton, a *metonymy,* when we fpeak of a thing by a
name different from its common one.

Ib. *Afmaceus-Cumeithus:* Men remarkable for their
compofitions: the one excelling in profe; the other in
poetry.

Pag. 96. *Leaving,* &c.   Arab. *Depofiting, or fixing
on my heart (gamra-'l-gáda) fierce burning coals:* a proverbial form, fignifying the great anxiety any one labours under.   *Gádan,* is the name of a tree, the
wood of which produces the moft lively burning coals.

ASSEM-

ASSEMBLY VI.

ENTITLED

MARAGENSIS.

HARITH Ibn Hemmam in one of his narratives gives us the following account of himself, saying : At *Maraga* I once happened to be present where there was a select company of learned men, reasoning and disputing about the subject of eloquence. One thing I observed, in which the most *accomplished scholars* among them mutually agreed : *viz.* That to the best of their knowledge there was not one man surviving, who had the talent of *making extempore verses :* and of altering them, so as that they might be agreeable in every respect to his own will and pleasure. Neither had their learned ancestors any person to succeed them, who was able to open *a new* and undiscovered *way* of instruction ; or to form such a *dissertation* as before had *not* been *attempted.* For instance, do but consider the best and most admired writers of this age, who are supposed to be masters of the *richest talents of eloquence*; and compare them with the learned men of ancient times : they will, I am persuaded, appear in a degree far inferior to them ; nay, though you esteem them to be as eloquent even as *Sehban Wajil.* In this assembly there was a man of an advanced age, sitting in a corner, among the crowd who had gathered together, like a number of clients or domestics that waited for protection. Whenever he perceived that the men *behaved* in a rude, indecent manner, either in speaking or in acting ; being too ready, from the little stock of learning they

had

had treafured up, to *declare* fome fentences that were
proper, but others of a contrary nature; he contracted his eye-brows, he curled his nofe, and *with* a
profound *filence* fixed his eyes on the ground, in fuch
a poſture as if he was ready to *ſtretch out his arms*:
drawing his body into a narrow compaſs as a camel, or an horfe does, before he begins his courfe,
that he may take larger fteps. You may likewife
compare him to a darter, who is fome time in pre-
paring his bow-ftring, that his arrows may have a
readier paffage. To a lion, or any other animal that
lies down in a *couching* pofture, defirous and eager
to purfue his prey. But when the company had *left
off difputing*, and recovered their fedate thoughts, after *the tumult* which was occafioned by their animofi-
ties had ceafed; fixing his eyes intenfly on them, he
addreffed himfelf to them in thefe words: If you are
defirous of knowing my fentiments, I muſt freely declare, the fubject you have been debating is of a difficult nature. And inftead of adhering to what indeed
is juftice and equity; you have deviated very much
from both. For what is the refult of your difcourfe? It
is this: Your praifes and encomiums have been enlarged in celebrating *dead writers*, who had no fpirit
nor vigour of eloquence to recommend them. And
fo immoderatly prejudiced have you fhewn your in-
clinations towards them, that in the moft ingrateful
manner you have brought low, you have reviled, you
have thrown contempt on the men of your own age.
Men, who are allied to you by birth, and with whom
you are connected by all the bonds of love and familiar acquaintance. You, who make fuch large pretences to *pure learning*, and refined eloquence! You,
who would be efteemed *maſters* of the moft *perfect
fcience!* What new invention have the *young genius's*
been able to produce? and in what fingle point of
literature hath this *prefent generation* exceeded thofe
of old time? Do thefe men explain and interpret
the fenfe of any difficult fubject, in a clearer and more
fignificant ftyle? Are the tropes and figures, that
                                        they

they ufe in their compofitions fet off and embellifh-
ed with more fweetnefs, and more agreeable entertainment? Are the treatifes they have publifhed, a-
dorned with more pleafing and exquifite beauties?
Or the poetry they have written, with thoughts more
lofty and fublime than thofe of ancient poets? But
to confider things in a proper manner; let me put
this queftion : Was the fenfe and underftanding of
our predeceffors fuperior in any refpect, to that of
the *vulgar and common herd* of mankind; from which
nothing could be produced that was either *fublime or
elegant?* they have indeed been celebrated as men of
high merit, and worthy to be imitated, becaufe of
their fuperiority in age : but not on account of any
excellency to which they had *a real and juft title.* One
thing with regard to the prefent times, I am well fatisfied of, that the chief and principal intention of a
perfon who undertakes to write poetry, is, that his
compofition may be formed fo as to fhine like feveral
flowers differently variegated. When he would defcribe any fubject by way of metaphor, he takes as
much pains to change and diverfify his words, as the
inhabitants of *Jemáma* do, in mixing the colours of
their garments. If his thoughts are employed in making fome new difcovery, *the produce* fhall be of more
importance than what he expected. In labouring to
make the fenfe of his orations ftrong and compendi-
ous ; they appear fo weak and imperfect, that no
one is defirous of imitating them. When he would
diftinguifh himfelf by fome extempore performance ;
inftead of meriting applaufe, you rather wonder, and
are aftonifhed at his impudence. And if he attempts
any thing unufual, which hath not been fo much as
heard of ; all his efforts prove languid and feeble.

After thefe reflections, a certain perfon who prefided in the council, to whom the utmoft refpect was
paid as the *principal*, of the higheft quality of this affembly, made this reply : Who is this man that
takes upon him to difcover and *folve* the greateft difficulties, exerting his authority in fuch an arbitrary,

heroic

heroic ftyle? To which he anfwered, I am the man
who hath delivered himfelf with that freedom; prepared to enter the ftage, and engage with thee in the
fharpeft combat. And if thy inclination prompts thee,
give the challenge, provoke, call upon, contend with
him. He is ready in every circumftance to make thee
full fatisfaction. The anfwer made to this was, You
are to confider, Sir, that in our country we know the
nature of birds fo well, as not to fet the fame value
on the *worft fpecies of kites*, that we do *on the vultur*,
or the eagle. Neither are we fo ftupid but we can readily diftinguifh *fragments of filver from pebble ftones.*
And indeed as there are very few, whofe circumftances have been mean and calamitous, that *have been
raifed* to any eminent ftation of dignity and honour:
fo thofe who *have fignalized themfelves* by their heroic
exploits, have not encouraged others to imitate them;
but inftead of that, would be thrown into the utmoft
confufion, even at the fight of a deftroying enemy.
Let me then advife thee not to make thyfelf ob-
noxious to cenfure, nor to expofe thy reputation to
one who is able to detect and make public the weaknefs of thy underftanding. And when thou art inftructed by a candid monitor, inftead of fhewing the
leaft averfion, hear him with the ftrongeft attention.
All the anfwer he made to this, was, It is incumbent
on *every man* to know the ftrength of his own genius.
But it will not be long before thefe *difficult points* be
made clear and obvious.

After this the affembly entered into a very deep
confultation, what method they fhould take to *fatisfy
themfelves of the depth of this man's underftanding*; and
to know, from the ftricteft and moft accurate examination, by what means he had attained to that faculty of expreffing himfelf, in fo eafy and ready a
manner. This confultation being ended, one of the
company faid, Deliver him up to me, that I may
take my chance, and try if I cannot undertake the
fame weighty and difficult conflict, in which I was
once engaged. A conflict of the moft intricate nature;

ture; the defign of which was, *To open the brighteft vein* of wit and judgement; and to difplay in the moft expeditious way, all the elegancy and beauty of language. They then readily complied, and *entrufted to him* the whole management of this affair, and gave him equal power with that which the *Chawárigi* conferred on *Abu Naúma*. No fooner did they confent to his propofal, but he immediately directed himfelf and his difcourfe to this old man, who prefided in the affembly; and faid: As I am fo fortunate to affociate with one who is the principal man of the company, I fhall be very careful how I exprefs myfelf; and as folicitous in embellifhing my words, and fetting them off to advantage, as a woman is in appearing with all her jewels and fplendid ornaments.

In the city which I inhabited, when my family was fmall, I was able in fome meafure, to fupport myfelf with the income I was poffeffed of. But as they increafed and became *more numerous*, and *my fubftance* was exhaufted, I left my own country, and applied myfelf to one with the higheft expectation of having *a fupply* for my great neceffity. He, I muft confefs, received me with the utmoft alacrity and benevolence imaginable; and at *all times* and feafons I was fure of a ready affiftance: I then made my requeft to him that he would permit me to return to the place from whence I came, as I had met with fuch *chearful reception*, and fo much generous treatment. But to this he replied, It is my full and determined refolution by no means to difmifs thee, furnifhed with provifions and what elfe is neceffary for a traveller; neither will I repair thy diffipated fubftance, nor reftore thee to thy native country, only upon this condition, that before thou takeft leave of us, thou wilt draw up in particular form, and commit in writing an exact account of thy condition and circumftances, and depofite it with us to be kept as a lafting memorial. This epiftle or writing muft confift of words that fhall be read alternately, fome with the *ufual points*, others, that have them not. The impofition was attended
with

with fo much difficulty, that with the greateft patience
for no lefs than a whole year, I *ftudied* how I might
accomplifh it ; but to no purpofe, or to any real fatisfaction. During all that time my endeavour was
to keep my *thoughts* intenfly employed ; and yet inftead of vigilance, I found I was affected with an
higher degree of ftupor. I was then folicitous to have
the affiftance of fuch as were efteemed learned and celebrated authors. But fo far from receiving fatisfaction I found they difcouraged me, by the contraction
and aufterity of their faces, and turned themfelves
from me, as not willing, if it had been in their power,
to help me. But one of the company faid, If what
thou haft alledged in thy behalf is in every refpect
confiftent with real fact and truth ; by fome token
or other, I defire thou wilt give us full and unexcep-
tionable conviction. To this he replied : Thy requeft
to me is fuch that I am as ready to grant it, as a
fwift horfe is to purfue his courfe when the rider urges
him to it. Or by way of comparifon, Thou defireft
a river would overflow it's banks to water the earth,
when it hath already fpread itfelf far and wide to refrefh the barren, thirfty ground. Thou haft *committed
the truft* to one who knows how to manage it. And
given the province to him who will govern it to the
beft advantage. From a very deep and attentive confideration, (like a man after a fatigue, his ftrength
having been much exhaufted) he *recovered his fpirits*, and
reduced his faculty to it's ufual copioufnefs : faying,
Prepare thy ink and other proper materials, and write
as I dictate to thee.

" A generous difpofition [may the divine profperity accompany thee !] is one of the higheft ornaments we can attain to. But as to a narrow, felfifh
temper, [may fortune caft a fhade on his eyes, who
envies thee !] nothing is more inftrumental in debaf-
ing a man's character. A man of true courage is a
terror to his enemy; and hath a juft reward : but a
coward who deceives you, is like a fire-pan, that, take
never fo much pains, gives you not one fpark of fire.

An

An hofpitable man, one, whofe generofity multitudes partake of, receives you with pleafure whenever you want refrefhment: but a covetous churl defrauds you of what in juftice you are entitled to ; and like a barren foil ; inftead of fhewing any compaffion, terrifies you by the difappointment of finding no relief in your greateft extremity. He who difpenfes his favours *with eafe* and chearfulnefs, *fupports* you in the *genteeleft manner*. But a man of a morofe, *quarrelfome* temper, purfues all poffible meafures to *vex and difturb you*. A bounteous gift to a perfon in diftrefs alleviates the circumftances of his mifery : but he who turns his back on your complaints, leaves you involved in troubles, which like fo many branches of trees join themfelves to each other. Gratitude in the ftrongeft, fincereft terms wifhes the happinefs of benefactors, that divine bleffings may attend them, and deliver them from the calamities of life : and even a covetous man, fhould a fpirit of bounty rife in him, merits general commendation, and wafhes away the ftains of his former fordid difpofition. A man of a candid, ingenuous temper, freely acknowledges the kindnefs of his friend, and is defirous, to the utmoft of his power, of making fome recompence. He who refufes you a good office, when he is able to do it, brings upon himfelf ignominy and difgrace. To difregard any thing devoted to facred purpofes ; or to violate any duty that we are obliged to pay to a wife, a family, an acquaintance, a man of dignity and honour ; is an inftance how much we err from the rules of piety and decorum : and to difappoint fuch as have *raifed their expectations* of fuccefs in an affair of importance, is a crime of an heinous nature. No one is of a tenacious, fraudulent difpofition, without difcovering his want of judgement : but he who is not of that temper, treats you with the higheft juftice. A man who is very folicitous in heaping treafure upon treafure, deferves the character both of a mifer, and a defpifer of religion : for he who is pious and good, is *bounteous and liberal*.

H
k

When

When in points of difpute thy advice is required, let it determine the controverfy. And where fome things are really blameable, let thy courteous behaviour connive at them. If a poor object petitions thee for relief with a cloudy, dark countenance, do thou *look upon* him with a pleafing face, and enrich him with prefents. Give no occafion even to thy enemies to reproach thee; but rather to commend thee for thy civil treatment. Is thy family diftinguifhed for their fteddinefs, and regular conduct? this will be a means of *repelling* the infults of an adverfary. A man in an honourable ftation, by his generofity *raifes* to himfelf a tower of glory. Should any one in diftrefs implore thy aid; fend him not away *empty*. Does he celebrate thy due praife; let him not lofe his reward. Let thy generofity refrefh the indigent; and thy plenteous *fhowers* defcend on them. So far from laying any reftraint on thy bounty, let it flow in full ftream, like milk from the camel. And if through parfimony, thou art inclined to reject a neceffitous object, fuffer not fuch a temper to prevail. It is my earneft defire that thou wouldeft weigh well the perfon who places his hope and confidence in thee: he is an old man, in the decline of life. What fhall I compare him to? even to a fluctuating afternoon fhadow, when the fun is haftening to go down to his place. And what is worfe, he hath no aid, no fupport to depend on. His intention of coming to thee, was from the opinion he had conceived of thy goodnefs: and fo forcible this intention! that it *urged him* with all the power imaginable. He therefore felected the beft and choiceft flowers of eloquence, and fcattered them in the encomiums he hath beftowed on thee. To render what is due to thee he thought himfelf in juftice obliged. But as to thofe things for which he petitions, they are of fmall confequence. They require not much time to be examined; for the reafons why they call for thy affectionate benevolence, why they hope for grace and favour, are very plain and evident. Thus did he not only praife what was truly com-

commendable, but object againſt what was blame-worthy. And no wonder that his commendations were admired, and received with applauſe ; and his obejections with much diſtaſte. But notwithſtanding this different treatment, a conſiderable number of domeſtics preſſed upon him, like thoſe who to quench their thirſt, preſs upon one another, ſtriving who ſhall firſt drink of the ſpring : domeſtics, by the decline of fortune labouring under the moſt piercing difficulties ; deſtitute and naked as birds that have *no feathers* on their wings ; all involved in a ſqualid, miſerable con-dition. But as to himſelf, the flood of tears that iſſued from him, was ſo great as to confirm every particular he had delivered to them. His conſternation ſo ſtrong, that he was like a perſon at once deprived of his ſen-ſes, to ſuch a degree, that there ſeemed not only a diſſolution of mind, but of the body likewiſe. So tur-bulent his *cares*, that they enter and take poſſeſſion of him with the ſame eagerneſs that weary travellers do of an inn or place of entertainment, by no means to be diverted or excluded, till they are quite *refreſhed*. His countenance ſo pale, as to exceed the common appearance of ſuch as labour under long ſickneſs, and are even at the point of death : or ſuch as meet with unexpected diſappointments, having raiſed their hopes to the higheſt degree of ſucceſs. His fortunes being entirely diſſipated, like camels without a keeper, he wanders from place to place, till *old age* and *grey hairs* macerate and emaciate him. The enemy he contends with *tears to pieces* his character. The eaſe and tranquility he uſed to enjoy is taken from him, and ſent into baniſhment. But notwithſtanding he is deprived of ſo much comfort, his deſire is not ſo in-tenſly fixed on recovering it, as to ſhake his conſtan-cy, or provoke any perſon's indignation againſt him : neither are his *thoughts* ſo *corrupted*, as to want ſevere methods to reform them. When *any one* hath juſt reaſon to complain of the hardſhips he undergoes, he is not to be blamed. And no eminently diſtinguiſhed alliance ſhould be turned to hatred or diſeſteem. But

ſuffer

suffer not thy high station to violate thofe facred
rights which neceffarily belong to it. Do not therefore *fruftrate his expectations* of having relief from his
anxiety by a liberal and chearful donation. Juft reafon then he will have to fpread thy fame; and celebrate thee among thofe men with whom he fhall at
any time converfe. My fincereft wifhes are, That
thy life may be of long continuance : that deftruction
of every kind may be removed far from thee ; that
riches may increafe fo as to enable thee to be affectionate and bounteous : that a proper remedy may
never be wanting to difpel all forrow and anxiety :
nor a true friend, to folace thee when thy years are
advancing, and old age feizes thee. It is likewife my
earneft defire, That the neceffary conveniences of life
may never fail thee : that thy joys may be youthful
and vigorous : and that no limits may be fixed to
thy generous conduct fo long as the rich man's hofpitable manfion is frequented ; or the repulfe of an
inhuman, fordid wretch is dreaded. And with this
let me conclude.

Having finifhed this excellent and ufeful difcourfe ;
and given the audience a very fatisfactory proof to
how great a degree he was *mafter of* a polite and eloquent ftyle ; the affembly not only complimented him
with their higheft praifes , but gave ample teftimony
of their approbation by facts as well as words : for
their benevolence and generofity to him was fo free
and affluent, that they ftrove which of them fhould
be moft diftinguifhed. After this they defired to know
from what branch or family he was defcended : what
the particular feat or place of his habitation ? to which
he replied :

> *In line direct from Perfian family,*
> *Gaffan by name, of royal progeny,*
> *Pure and from mixture free is my defcent,*
> *A native of* Serugium, *that juftly boafts*
> *Of it's unparallel'd antiquity.*
> *My family of higheft dignity !*

- *Splendid*

Splendid in ev'ry branch, like to the sun,
When the most beauteous aspects he assumes.
A seat so pure, so delicately plac'd,
As to be guarded from infectious air.
By nature and by art so well contriv'd,
That paradise itself cannot excel.
How happy was the time, I then enjoy'd!
How perfect ev'ry pleasure of my life!
With what complacency, what ease of mind,
Did I the paths of verdant meadows tread!
In all my projects sure to find success.
Those were my glorious, my triumphant days,
When with the glitt'ring ornaments of youth,
I shone in brightest splendour; no eclipse!
And fortune smil'd with all her beauteous charms.
Various, 'tis true, the motions she pursues!
Her smiles too often chang'd to angry frowns!
And such events, tho' ignominious,
I saw without concern, or anxious thoughts.
But when the scene was alter'd, and my days
Of sorrow upon sorrow far advanc'd;
Such was th' oppressive load, that by th' excess,
If any one was ev'r deprived of life;
I must have fall'n a sacrifice to grief.
Or by redemption could my former days
Be once restor'd, my heart's most precious blood,
So far from being spar'd, should pay the price,
A treasure of such value to regain.
For as to death! were we to have our choice?
More eligible sure for man to die!
Than live, a troublesom, uneasy life,
Like beasts, to treatment base and vile expos'd.
Instead of pow'r their motions to conduct,
Dragg'd by a brazen ring fix'd to the nose,
They 're forc'd t' obey their cruel leader's voice,
Thro' difficulties tho' of the hardest kind.
Such man's condition, when in deep distress!
More eligible sure for man to die,
Than live to see those of the noblest rank,
Insulted by the lowest, meanest class

Of

Of such as are the objects of contempt.
If you enquire, to what must we impute
These seemingly irregular events?
To fortune's obstinacy you'll charge the crime.
For if her conduct was not so perverse;
If all our days were clear and undisturb'd
With clouds that intercept our fullest sight;
The inconveniencies of life that rise
From those of evil genius, would remove.
Were all her motions steddily pursued,
And all her favours equally dispers'd!
How sure, how even ev'ry stage of life!
No apprehensions of a sudden change!

He then proceeded in his narrative to speak of the
governor, who had been so *very generous* to him; and
given him this charge, to addres himself to those who
would take him under their protection; and by whose
interest he might be preferred to the office of *Diwan,
public register,* and *dictator of public epistles.* But instead of applying to them for such preferment, he
was entirely satisfied with the presents they had made
him; and with a kind of noble disdain refused to ac-
cept of the employment which was proposed to him.
The author of the narrative [*Haririus*] said, I must
acknowledge *I knew* very well who the person was
[*Abuzeid*] before he produced such specimens of his
eloquence; and by some intimations had in a manner shewn of how great esteem he was before he *had
displayed* himself in so shining a light: but by the motion of his eye-lids he signified to me, *not to make* any
discovery of him. He then left the company loaded
with their *bounteous rewards*; and removed like a
victorious conqueror with his rich spoils. I followed
him very closely, paying him all the respect and civility that in justice he deserved. But I could not help
blaming him with some passion for refusing the office
of *Diwan.* He, instead of giving me a direct answer,
turned himself suddenly with a facetious smile, and
repeated the following verses in an entertaining mu-
sical tone.

I.

To travel diſtant countries,
Tho' poverty diſtreſs me,
Hath always been my option ;
Rather than be ſubſiſted
In one fix'd habitation,
By gen'rous contributions.

II.

For by a long experience,
And private obſervation,
I've ſeen th' inſulting treatment,
I've heard the rough expreſſions,
Of provinces chief rulers.
How grievous their expreſſions !

III.

So partial are their favours !
So prejudic'd their judgement !
That the reward they give you,
Fruſtrates your expeƈtations.
Like thoſe who form a building,
But leave it quite unfiniſh'd.

IV.

Permit me then t' adviſe thee,
Never to be deluded
With ſpecious, vain pretenſions ;
Thoſe treacheries of fortune !
Nor to attempt explaining
Obſcurities myſterious:

V.

For ev'n the higheſt pleaſures,
Which take ſuch ſtrong poſſeſſion
Of all our thoughts, when dreaming ;
Soon as the ſlumber ceaſes,
By ſudden fear and terror
Quite diſappear and vaniſh.

H 4

NOTES

NOTES

ON

ASSEMBLY VI.

ENTITLED

MARAGENSIS.

PAG. 107. *Maragenſis*. This *Aſſembly* takes it's name from *Maràga*, a city in Perſia, one of the metropoles of *Adſerbeijani*: remarkable not only for it's plenteous produce, pleaſant gardens, &c. but for men of learning and great genius's. Vid. *Ind. Geogr*. annexed to the *life of Saladin*, by *Schultens*. There is another *title* which this *Aſſembly* claims, viz. *al-chaiſáo*: a word that intimates different colours ; and applied to a perſon who hath one eye *gray*, and another *black*. It is ſo called becauſe of the various matter of it's compoſition.

Ib. *Accompliſhed ſcholars*. Arab. *Knights of the pen, and princes of eloquence* ; including both orators and poets, endowed with a peculiar firmneſs and ſtrength of mind.

Ib. *Making ext. verſes*: Arab. *Compoſing with great readineſs pure poetry: or, drawing marrow from the bone*.

Ib. *A new way: Tarìkaton gárron: a way diſtinguiſhed by a white mark*: applied to *true eloquence*, which in the Arabic phraſe appears with a candid, fair mark on her forehead. The character of a Faithful Mahometan, is deſcribed in the hiſtory of *Timur*, p. 3. *cóllo agár-rin*

rin mohággalin : every one who is diftinguifhed by a white mark on his forehead and on his feet.

Ib. *Differtation,* &c. The ftyle of the Arabic here, we may fay with *Schultens,* is very bold : for the *differtation not attempted,* is compared to *a virgin not defloured.* But it is in frequent ufe with Arabic writers ; the comparifon of a *virgin* being applied to any noble fubject, when the flower and dignity of it is fuch as hath not been cropt, or treated of by other writers. *Thou art not the firft Author of this oration :* literally, *Thou art not the Mafter of this oration's virginity.*

> *Avia Pieridum peragro loca, nullius ante Trita folo.* Lucretius.

Vid. *Schultens* Not. ad *Excerpta ex Ifpahanenfi.* p. 14.

Ib. *Richeft,* &c. Arab. *Who have it in their power to hold and moderate the reins of eloquence.*

Ib. *Appear,* &c. Arab. *Like fo many fcholars, or clients that depend on the inftructions of their mafters, or the advice of their counfellors.*

Ib. *Sebban Wajil.* Vid. Not. on *Affemb.* V. p. 97.

Ib. *Behaved,* &c. Arab. *Exceeded their bounds fo as to be carried beyond the limits of their courfe.*

Pag. 108. *Declare,* &c. Arab. *Difperfe from their little bafket dates both good and bad.*

Ib. *With filence,* &c. *Muchránbik.* A proverbial expreffion, fignifying the pofture of one, who as occafion offers is ready to take his flight : and applied to him who is filently contriving fome mifchief.

Ib. *Stretch out his arms : Li-janbáa.* A word appropriated to a ferpent that fixes his eyes on the ground, with an intention *to leap fuddenly on his prey ;* in the fame fenfe with *átraka :* by which *Taábbeta Sjérrán* defcribes an artful, mifchievous man, viz.

> *When on the ground his eyes intenfly fix,*
> *He fpreads his venom like the morning dew.*
> *Such is the pofture of the Bafilifk,*
> *Dire poifon fcattering in every place.*

Ib.

Ib. *Couching: Rábidon.* A word corresponding with that in the Hebrew, *Gen.* xlix. 9. " Judah is a lion's whelp: from the prey, my son, thou art gone up. He ftooped down, *rabatz, he couched* as a lion." There is a peculiar beauty in the fame expreffion as applied to *Cain, Gen.* iv. 7. " If thou doft not well, SIN *robetz, lieth* at the door." i. e. *Coucheth,* in readinefs, as it were, to feize thee for his prey.

Ib. *Left off difputing.* Arab. *When they had emptied their quivers.*

Ib. *Tumult,* &c. Arab. *When the tempefts were calmed.*

Ib. *Dead writers.* Arab. *Putrefied, rotten bones.*

Ib. *Pure learning: Al-nákda: Coin not adulterated.* From *nákada: He pierced the drachma.* i. e. He tried whether it was made of good metal.

Ib. *Mafters: Mawabidhato:* A Perfic word, appropriated to the *chief of the Magi.*

Ib. *Of the moft perfect fcience.* Arab. *Of loofing and binding.*

Ib. *Young genius's.* Arab. *New fprings, or bubbles of genius.*

Ib. *Prefent generation.* The Arabic alludes to the *hippodromus:* with this queftion, viz. *Wherein does the horfe of the age of two years, excel that of five years?* A proverbial form of fpeaking, applied to the different talents of men of different ages.

Pag. 109. *Superior to vulgar,* &c. Arab. *Clearer than thofe watering-places where cattle go to drink, and with their excrements difturb fo as that nothing appears but mud and filth.*

Ib. *Sublime and elegant.* The Arabic here refembles the compofitions of the Ancients to *wild beafts:* as if they were loofe and irregular, not confined to any certain bounds : and which the authors formed not from their own genius, but patched together fuch collections as by accident they could meet with.

Ib. *A real and juft title.* Arab. Compares the ancient and modern writers with one perfon who *comes out of the water,* and another who is but juft *entered into*

into it : and that the latter may claim as much merit as the former.

Ib. *Jemáma.*   Vid. Not. on *Affemb.* V. p. 104.

Ib. *The produce,* &c. Arab. *When be digs deep for water,* inſtead of finding it, *he diſcovers a vein of gold.*

Ib. *Principal,* &c. Arab. *The eye of eyes.*

Ib. *Solve,* &c. Arab. *To break this hard ſtone.*   A proverb, intimating difficulties of the moſt abſtruſe kind.

Pag. 110. *Worſt ſpecies,* &c. A proverb, applied to the ignorant, and men of learning.

Ib. *Pebble ſtones, ſmall: Kíddaton : large, kadídon.* To expreſs the approach of a number of people, the Arabs ſay, They come *kiddaton wa-kadídon, both ſmall and great.*

Ib. *Have been raiſed,* &c. Arab. *Have placed themſelves as marks for darters.*

Ib. *Signalized themſelves,* &c. Arab. By experience raiſed *nakán, the duſt :* a word referring to the tumults of war.   From hence the Arab. Poet:

Should you in battle ſafe protection ſeek?
Friendly reception you are ſure to find :
Ev'n tho' [nakón] the duſt of death riſes ſo high,
That thickeſt darkeſt clouds condenſe the air.

Weddachus Ibn Iſmael, commending the bravery of his troops, writes :

But in the field of battle you may ſee
The bold-contending horſes cloth'd with [nakón] duſt :
Their riders like fierce demons rage and ſtorm
For ſpoil, which they in bounteous gifts conſume.

Ib. *Confuſion.* Arab. Points out thoſe who have never ſeen an engagement, and at the ſight of it would be in as much terror, as the eye is, when injured by ſtraw or duſt obſtructing the ſight.

Ib. *Every man,* &c. Arab. " Every man beſt knows the mark of *kidhko, ſagittæ aleatoriæ, his arrow of chance.* A proverb, intimating, *Every one is*
beſt

beſt acquainted with his own condition." One of the ſuperſtitions of the Arabians before *Mahomet*, was, to inſcribe particular marks on *arrows* ; to mix them together, and to draw them out, that they might know what good or bad fortune would attend them. Vid. *Pocock.* Not. on *Abul Faraj. Specim. Hiſt. Arab.* p. 328. This cuſtom of divination was ſtrictly prohibited by *Mahomet. Alcor.* ch. v. v. 4. and v. 99. Comp. *Ezek.* xxi. 21. The king of Babylon ſtood at the parting of the way, to uſe divination : *he made his arrows bright.*

Ib. *Difficult points.* Arab. *The night will ſoon diſappear by the approach of the morning.*

Ib. *Satisfy themſelves,* &c. Arab. *To probe, as a ſurgeon does the wound, the depth of his inexhauſted well.*

Pag. 111. *Open the brighteſt vein,* &c. The Arabic compares the means uſed to find out what was true wit and judgement, to the *Lydian ſtone,* which was applied to diſcover genuin from adulterated gold.

Ib. *Entruſted,* &c. Arab. *They inveſted him with the dignity of a ſponſor.*

Ib. *Chawárigi,* or *Karegites, ſeparatiſts.* The principal leader of theſe men for twenty years, was *Katri Temimenſis,* ſurnamed *Abu Naâma,* from the horſe he uſed to ride on : and called *naáma,* becauſe, in ſwiftneſs he exceeded an *oſtrich,* which in Arabic is *Naâ-'mah.* The *Karegites* revolted and made an inſurrection againſt *Ali,* the fourth *Caliph* from Mahomet. Vid. *Ockley's Hiſt. Sarac.* vol. 2. p. 50. edit. 1757. They were reckoned heretics, maintaining that in this world, there was no neceſſity of a ſuperior power, or *Imâm,* a name peculiar to Mahomet. Vid. *Ab. Phar. Hiſt. Dyn.* p. 170. Read more of this ſect and their tenets : *Sale's Prelim. Diſc.* to his tranſlation of the *Coran.* p. 173.

Ib. *More numerous.* Arab. *More weight was laid on my ſhoulders. One of light ſhoulders,* proverbially, is, *a man who hath neither family nor riches.*

Ib. *My ſubſtance exhauſted.* Arab. *My ſmall rain or dew dried up.*

Ib,

Ib. *A supply*. Arab. *Refreshing the splendor of my countenance.*

Ib. *At all times*. Arab. *He assisted me both morning and evening.* Vid. Not. *Ass.* I. on *Excursion*, p. 11.

Ib. *Chearful reception*, &c. The Arabic by a bold figure compares his *desire of returning*, to *riding on the back of alacrity*.

Ib. *Usual points*, &c. What our Author means, is, that the words to be used in that *epistle* or *writing*, must alternately be such as are marked with the *diacritical points*, and with others not so distinguished. For whosoever is acquainted with the *Arabic alphabet*, knows, that there are *fifteen* letters with, and *thirteen* without those marks.

Pag. 112. *I studied*, &c. Arab. *I cultivated, or made suit to my eloquence, so as to bring it to maturity, but received not the least answer.*

Ib. *My thoughts*, &c. Arab. *I kept my genius awake.*

Ib. *A river would overflow*, &c. Proverbially used when we ask a favour, and there is no necessity for asking it.

Ib. *Committed the trust*, &c. Proverbially, *Thou hast given the bow to him who knows how to polish it:* intimating, that an eloquent man is best qualified to speak in public.

Ib. *Given the province*, &c. A proverb of the same kind: Arab. *Thou hast given the house to it's builder.*

Ib. *Recovered his spirits*. Arab. *Meditated even till his spring (exhausted) recovered it's vein,* i. e. his paternal genius.

Ib. *Reduced*, &c. Arab. *Recalled his milch-camel to her usual discharge of milk.* In commendation of an eloquent man, the Arabians say, *How plenteous is the flow of his milk!*

Pag. 113. *With ease*, &c. Arab. *Smoothly, and without knots.*

Ib. *Supports you*, &c. Arab. *Feeds, or supplies the mouth with nourishment.*

Ib. *Quarrelsom*. Arab. *Hurts your eye with a straw,* or *mote.* *Straws in the eye*, figuratively express *vexa-*

tion

tion, and *pain*. For inſtance: *My poverty gave him as much pain as if a ſtraw was in his eye. A man of courage can not bear a ſtraw in his eye:* i. e. *He is never eaſy till he hath avenged himſelf of his adverſary. He ſhuts both his eyes, having ſtraws in his eye-lids:* i. e. *He labours under great difficulties. They raiſed mine eye to it's ſight, after I had contraƈted the eye-lids by the burning pain of the ſtraw:* i. e. *They refreſhed me after my great afflictions.* To the ſame purpoſe, *A generous man, if your eye is injured by a ſtraw, removes the blemiſh ſo as that it cannot be ſeen. A ſtraw in the eye,* is by the Arabians applied in the ſame ſenſe with that which our Saviour, *Mat.* vii. objeƈted to the Jews. Thus the Arab. Poet writes:

> *Fix'd in Thine eye is evidently ſeen*
> *A tranſverſe beam, th' impediment of ſight:*
> *And yet to thy obſervance it is ſtrange,*
> *That Mine's obſtruƈted by the ſmalleſt ſtraw.*

Ib. *Raiſed their expeƈtations,* &c. Arab. *Sons of hope.*
Ib. *Bounteous,* &c. Arab. *Does not contraƈt the hollow of his hand. Contraƈting and opening the hand,* being oppoſite terms to covetouſneſs and liberality. Thus the Poet *Zohair* ſpeaks in praiſe of a generous man:

> *So uſed to ſtretch and open wide his hand,*
> *That to contraƈt it, 'twas in vain to ſtrive:*
> *For ev'ry finger ſtrong reſiſtance made.*

Vid. verſ. 8. Carm. Tograi.

Pag. 114. *Look upon,* &c. Arab. *Let thy moon ſhine upon him.*
Ib. *Repelling,* &c. Arab. *A ſharp ſword will deſtroy them,* i. e. in the Eaſtern ſtyle, *Steddineſs in a family reſiſts hoſtilities:* but *if the edge of the ſword is blunt,* i. e. *If the family is at variance with one another,* there ariſes great confuſion.

Ib.

Ib. *Raifes*, &c. Arab. *Honour builds*, i. e. A good character rifes by degrees like a ftately edifice.   Thus the Poet *Labidius :*

> *The building which our Anceftors contriv'd,*
> *Was form'd with fuch fuperior eminence ;*
> *That now their progeny, both old and young,*
> *To mount the higheft fummit are prepar'd.*

Ib. *Empty.* Arab. *Let him gather thy fruit:* A very rich man by the Orientals is frequently compared to a tree loaded with fruit.

Ib. *Showers.* Arab. *Let thy heavens,* or *thy fky fend forth rain,* i. e. Pour down thy favours on fuch as deferve them.

Ib. *Urged him,* &c. Arab. *His eager defire leaped.* Expreffing both the inward impulfe of his heart, and the outward motion of his body.

Pag. 115. *No feathers, and large plumes,* are applied by the Arabians to *poverty and riches.*

Ib. *Cares refreshed.* It is ufual with the Arabian Writers to compare anxieties and troubles with travellers much fatigued, and making as it were a forcible entrance into fome place of common reception : fuch were their *caravanferas,* built for the refrefhment of ftrangers.   Thus the Poet *Moleichus :*

> *When care approaches, like a trav'lling gueft,*
> *Free entertainment fhe is fure to find.*
> *With vigour ftrong, and with undaunted mind*
> *I bear the pain, tho' piercing as a fword.*

To the fame purpofe *Ommia :*

> *I feed the watchful hoft of all my cares,*
> *Let them attack me with their utmoft ftrength!*
> *Secure as if on camel's ftrongeft back,*
> *Tedious and dang'rous journies I purfue.*

Ib. *Old age, grey hairs,* &c. Thus the Poet *Ommia* defcribes family misfortunes:

4

Juft

Juſt as the Heir with long impatience waits
To ſeize th' inheritance of his father's wealth:
So by the ſame hereditary right,
The miſeries of fortune I poſſeſs.
Theſe make me old and grey before the time,
Conſume my body, and reduce my ſtrength.

Ib. *Tears to pieces.* Arab. *Fixes his tooth:* To bite and·devour him. The tooth is applied to any one who has it in his power to injure you. So our·Author, *Aſſemb.* 21.

Thus the viciſſitudes of fortune you'll prevent,
And with ſecurity defend yourſelf
From her diſtorted nail, and crooked tooth.

Again, ·*Collect.* ·*Hudel.*

No ſmall calamity from me expect,
Thou'lt feel the bite from it's diſtorted tooth.

Ib. *Thoughts corrupted.* The Arabic is a proverbial form, viz. *His wood is not corrupted, ſo as to be deſtroyed.* By *wood* the Arabians ſignify both the *inward* and *outward* condition of man. Thus our Author, *Aſſemb.* 21.

Tho' fortune preſs'd me hard, my wood remains
Firm with it's bark, not yielding to her ſtroke.

Aſſemb. 20. Speaking of one in great diſtreſs, he writes :

·*The vigour he poſſeſs'd, his wood robuſt,*
To ſpoil and weaken, Fortune never ceas'd.

Aſſemb. 30. Intimating the miſery of family-misfortunes :

Misfortunes various in their kind
·*My building, tho' of ſtone, attack'd,*
The ſplendid architecture's ſpoil'd :
The whole foundation much decay'd.
They've broke my wood ; but wo to him,
Whoſe branches by misfortunes fall.

Ib.

Ib. *Any one*, &c. Literally, *The breaſt that diſcharges it's obſtruction, is not to be blamed:* alluding to a proverb, viz. *It is not poſſible for a diſordered breaſt to avoid ſpitting;* ſignifying, That he who labours under adverſity, may be ſuffered to complain.

Pag. 116. *Do not fruſtrate his expectations,* Arab. *Make his hope white.* A *black* and a *white countenance,* in the Arab. ſtyle, are *a dejected and chearful* one.

Ib. *Maſter of,* &c. Arab. *How ſtrenuous he was in the conteſt of eloquence.*

Ib. *Serugium.* Vid. Not. *Aſſemb.* I. p. 17.

Pag. 117. *Tread the paths,* &c. Arab. *Draw the train of my long ſplendid robe.*

Ib. *Glittering ornaments.* Arab. *I prided myſelf in the garment of youth:* The flouriſhing ſtate of which is compared to a ſplendid robe, wrought with much art and ſkill. *A robe* or *garment* is a word which the Arabians apply to *life.* Thus, He took away his *garment of life:* i. e. He deprived him of life. From hence the Poet in *Hamaſa:*

> *What! tho' he wears the robe of life prolong'd;*
> *Yet 'tis not worth the name of honour's robe.*
> *The ſofteſt youth that glitters to the eye,*
> *Will ſoon be ſpoil'd of all his ſhining dreſs;*
> *Like ſlender reed expos'd to ev'ry blaſt:*
> *Verdant to-day, to-morrow quite decay'd.*

The ſofteſt youth: Arab. *The brother of ſoftneſs.*

Ib. *Nobleſt rank.* Arab. *Beaſts,* particularly *lions,* of the moſt generous breed.

Ib. *Meaneſt claſs.* Arab. *Hyænas.*

Pag. 118. *Very generous.* Arab. *Had filled his mouth with jewels.* Comp. *Pſal.* lxxxi. 10. *Open thy mouth wide, and I will fill it.*

Ib. *I knew,* &c. Arab. *I knew of what kind of wood his tree conſiſted before it's fruit was ripe.*

Ib. *Diſplay'd,* &c. Arab. *Before his moon had ſhone with ſuch ſplendor.*

Ib. *Not to make,* &c. Arab. *Not to draw the ſharp ſword from it's ſheath.*

I   Ib.

Ib. *Bounteous rewards.* Arab. *With his cloak-bag full and swelling.*

Pag. 119. *Partial favours.* Arab. *They do not rightly fit, or adjust favours,* so as to make them proper and acceptable to the person who receives them. The original literally compares such *favours* to *butter,* or any other ingredient which used to be put into leathern bottles; which ingredients perished, and came to nothing if the bottles were not well prepared to receive them. Comp. *Mat.* ix. 17.

Ib. *Deluded,* &c. Arab. *Be not deceived with a meridian shining vapour:* which by reflexion of the rays of the sun appears in the fields and sands a stream of water, but really is not.

A R A-

ARABIAN PROVERBS

IN THE SIX ASSEMBLIES.

               The

Assembly the Third.

Assembly the Fourth.

Assembly

TEXTS

TEXTS OF SCRIPTURE EXPLAINED.

F I N I S.

Lately publifhed, printed at *Cambridge*, and fold by
J. Johnfon and *B. Davenport*, and *Ben. White* in
London ; and *T.* and *J. Merrill* in *Cambridge* :

1 MR. Bally's Poem on the Juftice of the fupreme
    Being, 1s
2 ———————————— Wifdom of the fu-
    preme Being, 1s
3 ———————————— Providence of the fu-
    preme Being, 1s
4 Dr. Glynn's Poem on the Day of Judgment, 1s. 5th
    Edition
5 Dr. Porteus on Death, a Poetical Effay, 1s. 4th *Edition*
6 Mr. Lettice's Converfion of St. Paul, 1s
7 Mr. Zouch's Crucifixion, a Poetical Effay, 1s
    N. B. *The above Poems gained Mr. Seaton's Prize.*

8 The Traveller, an Arabic Poem, from the Latin of
    Dr. Pocock, by L. Chappelow, B. D. 1s 6d
9 Mr. Green's Tranflation of the Song of Deborah, 1s
10 ———————————— Prayer of Habakkuk,
    1s 6d
11 ———————————— Pfalms, 3s 6d
12 Mr. Bell's Differtation on the Caufes and Effects of
    the Populoufnefs of a Nation, 1s
13 Solomon de Mundi Vanitate, Lat. & Eng. à G. Bally
14 The Character of David, a Sermon by B. Porteus, D. D.
    6d. 2d *Edition*
15 A Caution againft religious Delufion, a Sermon by
    W. Backhoufe, A. M. 6d
16 St. Paul's Doctrine of Juftification by Faith, Three
    Difcourfes, by S. Hallifax, L. L. D. 1s 6d. 2d
    Edition
17 Remarks on feveral Paffages of Scripture, by M. Pil-
    kington, L. L. B. 3s
18 A Defence of the accented Pronounciation of Greek
    Points, by W. Primatt, A. M. 5s. *fewed*
19 Compleat Paradigms of the Hebrew Verbs, 1s
20 Dr. Law's Confiderations on the Theory of Religion,
    5th *Edition*, corrected and completed, 5s in *Boards*
21 Defcription of the Univerfity of Cambridge, with Views
    of the public Buildings, 2s
22 Happinefs, a Poetical Effay, by Mr. Meen of Emanuel
    College, 1s 6d
23 Newtoni Principia, cum Notis Variorum, 4to, 10s 6d
24 Poetical Epiftles to the Author of the New Bath Guide,
    1s 6d
25 Oratio F. Churchill, A. M. Aul. Clare

www.ingramcontent.com/pod-product-compliance
Lightning Source LLC
Chambersburg PA
CBHW021135020726
47500CB00003B/1094